CW00486954

When Dr Gavin Fletcher advertises his interest in Daisy Palmer by wearing a bunch of her name-sake flowers on a ward round, the Hartlake Hospital grapevine buzzes with a new romance. But have Daisy's romantic dreams any chance of coming true when Gavin seems to be such a determined bachelor?

SECOND-YEAR LOVE

BY

LYNNE COLLINS

MILLS & BOON LIMITED
London · Sydney · Toronto

First published in Great Britain 1982
by Mills & Boon Limited, 15–16 Brook's Mews,
London W1A 1DR

ISBN 0 263 73812 4

03/0382

Set in 10 on 12pt Times Roman

Photoset by Rowland Phototypesetting Ltd,
Bury St Edmunds, Suffolk.
Made and printed in Great Britain by
Richard Clay (The Chaucer Press) Ltd,
Bungay, Suffolk

CHAPTER ONE

DAISY was dreaming.

It was her besetting sin and she was often in trouble over it. Family and friends, teachers and employers, all had deplored her tendency to lapse into the rainbow world of dreams.

Yet she had done well at school and, later, at secretarial college. She had fretted for two years in routine office jobs, cheerful and capable, but bored, and one day she had roused from a reverie in the middle of coffee-break with the sudden inspiration to be a nurse.

She had taken to the training like a duck to water and felt immediately at home in the big, busy hospital, but she had still dreamed through some of her lectures in the days of Preliminary Training School.

Now she was dreaming on the ward.

Daisy stood by one of the long windows that overlooked the busy main road with its constant stream of taxis and red London buses, cars and motor-cycles, idly watching the pedestrians who chose to ignore the pelican crossing with its flashing lights and took their life in their hands whenever they attempted to cross from one side of the road to the other.

She loved the hustle and bustle of the great metropolis, with its drama and excitement and teeming millions, many of whom were destined to pass through the portals of the famous Hartlake Hospital at some time in their lives, if only to visit friends or relatives in one of the wards.

It seemed to Daisy that the hospital itself was like a big city, full of drama and excitement and activity. It was a world set apart from the one outside its walls. The atmosphere and the sense of urgency combined with its calm efficiency seemed to envelop her as soon as she entered from the busy street.

She remembered the very first time that she had mounted the wide stone steps and passed through the heavy glass doors into the main hall of the hospital, excited but apprehensive at the thought of the interview that would determine whether she was the right material for a Hartlake nurse. For Hartlake did not take just any girl who applied to their training school.

It was as selective as one might expect of a hospital whose nurses, like those of Guy's and Thomas's and Bart's, were known and sought after throughout the world. Hartlake was very jealous of its reputation and instilled pride and dignity as well as a comprehensive efficiency into its nurses.

Daisy remembered that Jimmy, the head porter, had known immediately that she had arrived for an interview in the hope of training as a Hartlake nurse.

He was an institution in himself. He had been at Hartlake for thirty years and prided himself on knowing every member of the staff by name and having a flair for instant diagnosis of each new patient who walked through the portals of Main Hall. He spent his leisure hours in reading medical text-books and journals and enjoyed long and informative talks with the medical students and had even been known to put them right on some knotty point with his superior knowledge. Jimmy was a character.

He had greeted Daisy with a warm smile and said that

he looked forward to seeing much more of her in the future. 'Hartlake is famous for its pretty nurses,' he had declared with a wink. 'They won't turn *you* down, miss . . .'

They hadn't, thankfully, but Daisy doubted if her pale blonde hair and cornflower blue eyes had influenced Matron or the Senior Sister Tutor.

Arriving that first day at the Preliminary Training School for six weeks of theoretical work in the classroom before going on to the wards, Daisy had felt like a very green girl for all her twenty odd years and wondered if she really wanted to be a nurse, after all. Then she found that the other girls in her set were suffering just as badly from an attack of last-minute nerves.

'Like a bevy of brides,' someone had said wryly, and the subsequent laughter had broken the ice and eased the tension.

The remark had been uttered by Joanne Laidlaw who had become Daisy's friend, sustaining her and bullying her through those weeks in P.T.S. when she had felt that she would never remember all that she was being taught and ought to have known better than to suppose she could ever qualify as a state registered nurse.

Cool, confident and competent, Joanne had sailed through preliminary training to emerge with flying colours—only to find that she became ill at the sight of blood when she began work on her first ward. Poor Joanne had wanted so badly to be a nurse, but she could not conquer that instinctive gut-reaction for all her efforts. Reluctantly, she had given up nursing to train as a physiotherapist. Still at Hartlake, she was Daisy's dear friend and trusted confidante and they shared a tiny flat in a tall, decaying Victorian house in one of the narrow

streets surrounding the hospital. Their friends declared
that they got on very well for all their difference of
temperament and tastes. It was true.

Now Daisy was in her second year of training and
while she still wore the traditional blue check frock of
the Hartlake student nurse, with its old-fashioned puf-
fed sleeves, she had exchanged the matching belt for a
plain blue one and she wore two blue stripes on the tiny
white cap that was perched so precariously on the blonde
plaits that she bound about her neat, shapely head. Her
hair was fine and silky and flyaway when it was loose; it
was often a problem to keep her cap in place, even with
the help of strategically-placed hairpins.

She had only meant to glance out of the window in
passing. But a tall, purposeful figure striding through the
stream of cars with complete unconcern for his safety
had caught her eye. She paused, and watched until the
stone pillars of the hospital frontage swallowed him up,
and then slipped easily into the most foolish of her
dreams.

Too many of her fellow nurses were in the habit of
weaving dreams about Gavin Fletcher. Too many of
them had made the mistake of responding to a certain
glow in his roving eye, only to be made very miserable
when it moved on to another pretty face or slender
figure. He was very careful of his safety when it came to
the dangers of romancing that might lead to the altar,
Daisy thought wryly. He was very attractive, very sure of
himself and seemed to be entirely without heart or
conscience.

She did not think that he had ever spoken to her
directly. Registrars did not notice very junior nurses—
not officially, anyway, and certainly not on the ward

within sight and sound of sister or the staff nurse in charge.

Fraternisation was not approved and Matron kept a close eye on her young nurses. Years of experience dating from her own early days on the wards had taught her that young doctors were very susceptible and quite unscrupulous in their pursuit of a pretty nurse. Most of them could not afford the time or the money for serious courtship, but there were plenty of opportunities for light-hearted romancing that could cause havoc among her nurses.

But for all Matron's vigilance, flirtation was rife. Hartlake, like any big teaching hospital, had its share of happiness and heartache among the staff. Nurses learned to be discreet and to carry on their affairs outside the hospital walls.

Daisy was sure that Gavin Fletcher did not know she existed. But in her delicious dream he did notice her and, falling in love in a moment, declared that he would take her away from all the routine drudgery of a nurse's life. Daisy nobly resisted the impulse of her heart and his fervent pleadings. Reminding him how much her patients needed her skill and caring concern and untiring devotion, she sacrificed their love to duty . . .

'You seem to have nothing to do, Nurse! May I suggest that Nurse Parkin could use another pair of hands in the sluice?'

Daisy jumped, hastily collecting her wool-gathering wits at the sound of that astringent voice. Sister Sweet was tall and slim and formidable, with a disposition that belied her name. She ran her ward on well-oiled and thoroughly well-scrubbed lines. Never wasting a moment of her busy day, she was quite determined that her nurses should not, either.

Daisy spun round, an apology forming itself hastily on her lips. *Yes, sister . . . sorry, sister* was an automatic response for any junior nurse who was being trained within an inch of her life!

She met the dancing eyes of Patti Parkin, who had caught her out before with that brilliant gift for mimicry. She laughed wryly. 'Another year's growth lost,' she reproached. 'One day Sister will catch you doing her work for her and I shall be delighted to see you get your come-uppance!'

Patti grinned, quite unrepentant. She had brought a breath of fresh air to Fleming, Men's Medical, with her lively personality and the mischievous sense of humour that matched her short auburn curls and bright green eyes and gamine prettiness. The men loved her. Even the most poorly patient would make an effort to respond to Patti's cheerful and always optimistic approach. The most gentle and instinctively thoughtful of student nurses, there were many of her seniors who predicted a very successful career for her in nursing if she was not whisked to the altar before she could finish her three years of training at Hartlake.

As the most junior of the first-year nurses on the ward despite her twenty-three years, having come rather later than most girls to nursing, Patti was general dogsbody. All the menial and most unpopular of chores fell to her lot. She took them all in her stride and no one ever heard her complain about the work, the patients, the long hours, her feet or anything else.

She was a boon and a blessing, Daisy thought grate-fully, whisking her off to help her with the never-ending rounds of pulse and temps, blood pressure and bedpans. Even Sister Sweet had been known to utter a word of praise for Patti while she scolded her in the same breath for taking much too long over a trivial task.

For while Daisy was a dreamer, Patti was a talker when patients needed cheering or stirring to greater efforts, or just the comfort of her bright voice filtering into a drug-induced drowsiness. She was also a very good listener and the kind of nurse who never seemed to be in a hurry, even if she had a hundred and one things to do. Sometimes she would be with a patient long after another nurse would have finished washing him or feeding him with a drinking-cup or entering his fluid intake and output on the chart.

Daisy liked her and they were friends, both on and off the ward. Second-year nurses did not often mix socially with a first-year in the early months of her training. But Patti was older and more sophisticated than most of her set and was more comfortable with friends closer to her own age. The five years between eighteen and twenty-three could be a lifetime of experience, she had been known to declare rather wryly. But she did not enlarge on that experience.

She worked hard, spending long hours with her books, studying and making notes and memorising the long lists of bones and nerves and muscles in the human anatomy. But she loved a party and she had enlivened many an evening in recent weeks, climbing into the Nurses' Home in the early hours through a ground-floor window, risking life and limb and Home Sister's wrath.

It puzzled Daisy that the attractive and warmly outgoing Patti turned down all the many invitations she received from the men she met. She was not interested, she insisted. She had come to Hartlake to nurse and she did not believe in playing with the fire that was meaning-less flirtation. Daisy could only admire her strength of mind when she saw how the men pursued her friend.

No one flirted with Daisy. For some reason, she only seemed to attract serious-minded young men who were aching to expound their pet theories on the endocrine tract or Meniére's disease or the treatment of diabetes mellitus. She had spent too many long evenings being a good listener, a polite smile pinned to her lips, while Joanne drifted dreamily to the music in the arms of her latest love and Patti laughingly protested her lack of interest in a persistent admirer.

Sometimes Daisy longed to be swept off her feet by a passionate and determined and devastatingly attractive man with nothing on his mind but the chemistry between the sexes!

Her thoughts had turned full circle and brought her unerringly back to Gavin Fletcher. She did not know what it was about him that she liked and admired. He was a rake and something of a rogue and he had a reputation that no sensible girl should ignore. It was really very foolish to remember a pair of dark eyes that had smiled without even seeing her, and to recall the way her heart had tumbled in her breast for no reason at all . . .

'You're in a dream this morning, Nurse,' Mr Benbow said reproachfully as she dried his arm before she had washed it. 'Thinking about your boy-friend, I suppose. Kept you out late last night, did he?' There was the hint of a leer in the rheumy blue eyes. Daisy smiled, soaped the flannel and reached for an arm. 'That's the one you've just done,' he told her with the sudden fretful impatience of the very old. 'Good job I've still got my wits! Some of you girls weren't born with *any*, seems to me!'

He was eighty-three and frail, but he was making a good recovery from an acute bronchitis. Sister had said that he was to be encouraged to wash himself, but he pleaded that it tired him. Daisy knew that he was trading on her good nature while Sister was busy with a pile of paper-work in the office. She suspected that his continued dependence on the nursing staff sprang from lonely old age and the fear that he would soon be sent home to his neglected council flat to take care of himself as ineffectually as before.

There were too many patients like Mr Benbow, and far too few beds and insufficient pairs of hands to care for them. But in fact he would shortly be sent to a geriatric unit and he would pass into the limbo of the forgotten.

Patients came and patients went on every ward. There was always a new face, a new name to remember, a new case history to absorb. It was essential to listen carefully to Report and to remember the notes scribbled hastily in a notebook or, sometimes, on the underside of her starched apron.

A good nurse was warmly concerned with every patient on the ward and tried to establish a friendly rapport with a few words. She knew that pain and anxiety and the indignity of illness affected people in different ways. There were good patients and there were difficult patients. There were patients who only stayed a few days and there were long-term patients.

But she must put them all out of her mind when she went off duty. She owed it to herself and to the patients and her colleagues to unwind, to relax, so that she came back to the ward feeling refreshed and able to cope with the many demands on her energy and emotions.

Daisy liked nursing. But it was hard work and demanding and sometimes she was discouraged. Some patients were totally unappreciative of all that was done for them. A nurse did not expect to be thanked; she was simply doing her job. But it helped to know that she had soothed pain or eased discomfort or relieved a burdened mind. Perhaps she was too sensitive.

It was not only the patients or the stern discipline of Sister Sweet or the routine chores of a medical ward. Some consultants could be brusque and sarcastic with the nursing staff for all the charm of the bedside manner that they bestowed on their patients. And there were times when Daisy caught her breath at the casual conceit of housemen and medical students who treated nurses as though they were a cross between a wardmaid and a doctor's delight!

She apologised to old Mr Benbow and applied herself with greater attention to washing him and assisting him into clean pyjamas and then settling him in an armchair in the Day Room.

Sister told her to prepare a bed for a patient who was being transferred from the Cardiac Unit for rest and observation. He was over the most dangerous time for someone who had suffered a heart attack and only needed nursing back to mobility and confidence.

She took a young man with a renal condition down to X-ray for an ultra-sonic scan and left him to hurry back to the ward to help with the mid-morning drinks and did not make the mistake this time of putting milk in the tea of a gall-bladder suspect who was in for observation and tests.

There was so much to remember and to observe and so many chores to be done . . . and so many little distractions and never enough time. Somehow, almost miraculously it seemed at times, they did get through the work and the ward ran smoothly and with apparent placidity. A nurse was never seen to run, but Daisy sometimes felt that she was running inside even if her feet moved at the accepted pace about the ward.

It was a very busy morning and she found that she had no time or opportunity for further dreaming. Sister saw to that!

She was sent to early lunch and she went thankfully, pushing through the swing doors of the ward without a glance for the tall man who was about to enter. She was hungry and her feet hurt and she was too used to white coats to look at them twice!

Gavin was not used to being ignored by the junior nurses. It could be irritating when they vied with each other for his attention on a ward, or nudged each other, giggling, when he passed them in a corridor. But there were times when it pleased him to take advantage of the impact of his good looks and charm on a pretty junior. Matron disapproved, of course. But that was part of the pleasure. Forbidden fruit had tasted sweet to a man since the days of Adam and Eve!

He paused with a hand on the door, looking after the trim-waisted girl with the shining blonde hair and a pair of slender legs that even black stockings and low-heeled black brogues could not mar, and wondered how he had come to miss this particular junior nurse.

'Nurse . . . !'

True to her training, Daisy turned obediently. Meeting the smiling dark eyes in that handsome and much too sensual face, she felt that sudden, alarming shock to her heart all over again.

'What did I do?' he demanded lightly with the smile that had spanned the great divide between a senior doctor and a junior nurse to such good effect in the past.

She was puzzled. 'Sorry . . . ?'

'You didn't smile. It's a sad day when a pretty girl passes by without a smile.'

His voice was deep and very pleasant and its slow drawl sent an odd little shiver of excitement along her spine. Or was it a certain look in the dark eyes that told her that a dream had come true to some extent. She had been noticed at last by this very attractive doctor.

But, remembering all the rumours about him, Daisy was not too sure that it was a good thing. Sometimes it was very much safer when a man didn't step out of a girl's romantic dreams to threaten her with a very physical reality!

'I didn't even see you, Dr Fletcher,' she said with perfect truth . . . and wondered that every instinct had not been alerted.

Tall, very attractive, an impressive man with his dark, crisply curling hair and smiling eyes and the charm that had been the downfall of too many girls if the hospital grapevine was to be believed, she usually knew with some mysterious sixth sense as soon as he walked into the ward, with or without a string of medical students in tow.

He raised an eyebrow. 'Invisibility has its uses, of course. But I do like to know when it's working.' He saw the hint of a smile in the rather lovely eyes and, encouraged, walked back to join her. 'You know my name. It's only fair that I should know yours, don't you think?'

In that foolish dream, too often indulged, Daisy had known just how to respond to such an approach, how to smile and what to say. Now, faced with an unexpected reality, she sought desperately for the words that would quicken and hold this man's fleeting and probably dangerous interest.

Joanne would know, she thought ruefully—and so would clever, quick-witted, amusing Patti! She was much too shy and too inexperienced and her heart was fluttering in her breast in a very odd fashion.

'Palmer,' she said carefully, a little reluctant and very cool because she was afraid of seeming too warm, too flattered, too ready to fall into his arms at a smile like so many girls. He was really much too attractive for his own good—or anyone else's!

'I can't believe that your parents didn't give you a first name,' he said, gently teasing.

She bit her lip. A little blush of an ancient embarrassment began to steal into her face. Through the years, she had grown used to the teasing and even ceased to worry about the reaction to her unusual name. Now, early dislike of it flooded her all over again together with a vivid recollection of horrid little boys who had pranced behind her on the way from school, chanting it to her discomfiture.

'Daisy,' she said, defiant.

Laughter welled in his dark eyes just as she had known it would. But it was not unkind amusement.

'I like it,' he declared. 'It's very pretty—and so are you. A tonic for the poor old boys on Fleming—*and* the not so old! Matron seems to be human, after all, despite all rumours to the contrary.'

'Not so human that she would approve of this conversation,' Daisy told him with a touch of spirit. He was too smooth, too sure of himself, too quick with his easy and meaningless compliments.

'In the shadow of the ward? Very true. We must continue it in rather more romantic surroundings, I think. Shall we make it the Kingfisher at eight o'clock?'

She almost smiled at the way in which he described the Kingfisher, the rather shabby pub across the road that was the haunt of some very doubtful characters as well as a great many of the hospital staff, as a romantic venue. But it was a popular meeting place. A little too popular, perhaps. It would be all over the hospital in no time if she met Gavin Fletcher for a drink in one of its crowded bars.

A quickening excitement was urging her to say yes. Common-sense warned her again about his reputation and told her firmly that she could never handle a man like this one who was noted for his sensuality and the charm which wore down a girl's resistance and the swiftness with which he tired and went in search of another conquest. It would be madness!

Bravely she resisted temptation. 'I'm sorry. I can't make it,' she said, letting him down lightly. She was a gentle girl who found it hard to rebuff any overture of friendship.

'Another date? How about tomorrow?'

She shook her head. 'No.' But she could not help being flattered by his persistence and her resolution was beginning to weaken before the smile in his eyes.

'Come on, girl. Just one drink. Where's the harm?' Gavin was persuasive. Girls liked to be coaxed, he knew . . . and they often said no the first time.

'I don't go out with doctors.' It was not quite true. She

should have said that she didn't go out with a doctor that she didn't trust.

He raised an amused eyebrow. 'We are men, you know.'

'Not my kind of men.'

His eyes danced. 'I can tell that you've had a wealth of experience,' he said, very dry.

'I shall miss lunch,' Daisy said, a little desperately and turned away . . .

CHAPTER TWO

HE had left the ward by the time she came back from a hurried and almost untouched lunch. Daisy was disappointed.

She would not have dared to speak to him while Sister Sweet was about to breathe fire at such a breach of etiquette, of course. And perhaps he would not have bothered to speak to her again. A man like Gavin Fletcher did not need to pursue an apparently reluctant girl when there were so many willing ones in his life.

Daisy knew she had been sensible. It would be very dangerous to encourage someone that she already liked too much without even knowing him. She responded much too readily to the glow in those dark eyes and the charm of his smile. She did not dare to dwell on what might happen to her at the touch of his hand.

The afternoon was as busy as the morning for Daisy and the other nurses, although there was less actual nursing involved. Sister went off-duty for a few hours, leaving Staff Nurse Trish King in charge. She was a good-natured, easy-going girl, but the work still had to be done and they did it with a slightly better grace because she did not chivvy them at every turn.

Visiting hours were eagerly awaited by the patients and it allowed the nursing staff to get on with some of the routine chores of the ward. Daisy was sent to check stock with Patti and they chatted happily as they counted sterile dressing packs and suture packs and gauze swabs and hypodermic needles.

The ward was thrown open to waiting relatives and friends. They came in rather cautiously, some shy, some apprehensive, some merely dutiful, clutching flowers and carriers containing clean pyjamas and bottles of squash. As soon as the kisses and other preliminaries were over, each patient settled down to talk about the ailments of the other patients with more interest than he temporarily felt in his own family or workmates.

A hospital ward was a world of its own. The outside world was very remote and the patients formed a close affinity with their fellows. They became fast friends and exchanged life stories, family trees and lengthy, detailed accounts of symptoms and what the doctor had said and what they had said to the specialist who finally admitted them for treatment. In very human fashion, they vied with each other for the honour of being a patient whose case had baffled all the experts . . . unless, of course, it happened to be true.

Usually, Daisy liked that hour in a busy afternoon when there was a rather more relaxed atmosphere on the ward. That afternoon, her head was full of Gavin Fletcher and she was torn between the impulse to turn up at the Kingfisher that evening at eight o'clock in the hope that he would be there—and the conviction that he had dismissed her without another thought when she turned down the invitation.

'. . . thirteen, fourteen! There, that's done!' Patti ticked off the last item on the list and smiled at Daisy. 'Five minutes before we do the teas,' she announced with a glance at the watch she wore pinned to her apron. 'Don't turn your back on old Mr Loftus, by the way.

He'll pinch your bottom just to prove to his brother that there's life in the old dog yet!' She laughed. 'He tried it on Sister – did you know?'

'I expect she blistered him for it,' Daisy said absently, tucking a strand of pale hair under her cap. Newly-washed, it was even more flyaway than usual.

'No. She actually smiled and said that she wouldn't trust him near any of her nurses. Teasing, you know— and the old boy was as pleased as punch! I rather liked her for it. She's as prickly as a porcupine but she does have some good points.'

'I suppose so.' Daisy's thoughts were far from Sister Sweet or old Mr Loftus and his kidney complaint.

'I should think he was very handsome when he was young,' Patti mused. 'A devil for the girls, too. He still has that glint in his eye. Oh, not like some old lechers. It's rather a nice glint. In a way, he reminds me of Gavin Fletcher.'

'Does he?' Daisy was non-committal, although the name had jerked her out of a reverie. She fiddled with her cap and a hairpin. The wretched thing was being more of a problem than it usually was, she thought crossly.

Patti glanced at her, a twinkle in her own eye. 'Like him, don't you?' she said gently.

Daisy tried not to stiffen. 'I don't know him,' she said, as carelessly as she could. It was absurd that the mere mention of his name could make her heart quicken and the blood race in her veins.

'As if that makes a difference! Who needs to know a man to fancy him?' Patti demanded in her direct way.

'I *don't* fancy him.' Daisy allowed the impatience with her unruly cap to break through, to colour the words.

Patti relented. 'I won't tease you,' she said penitently. 'It's rotten when you like someone who won't even look at you, I know.' It was the nearest she had ever been to a hint about her own past experiences with the opposite sex. Daisy did not even notice. 'Count your blessings, Daisy,' Patti went on wisely. 'He isn't the type that any girl who values her reputation should tangle with. People are still talking about Stella Grainger, after all.'

It was exactly what Daisy kept telling herself about Gavin Fletcher. But she did not like to hear it on anyone else's lips. It was obviously true that he could damage a girl's good name so badly that six months later the rumours about their relationship were still going the rounds. Daisy tried not to listen to them. She did not believe that any doctor or staff nurse could be so irresponsible as to make love in the ward office where anyone might discover them. It was rumoured that Matron had caught them, but Daisy felt that it *was* only rumour. Certainly Stella Grainger had left suddenly, but it could be for the family reasons that she had claimed.

'Sometimes I think a lot of nonsense is talked about him,' she said with sudden impatience. 'Give a man a bad name and he'll do his best to live up to it! I don't suppose that Gavin Fletcher is so very bad as everyone declares. He may be quite nice.' Very feminine pride suddenly motivated her to add: 'He has looked at me, actually. He asked me out but I wasn't interested.'

Patti believed the impulsive claim. For Daisy was a pretty girl and it would be more surprising if Gavin Fletcher had not taken an interest in her. As for refusing to go out with him, it was just what she would have expected. Daisy was rather shy and not very experienced and she would feel out of her depth with a man who was reputed to be a Casanova. Patti knew that Daisy liked him. Shrewd and perceptive and fond enough to be concerned, she had noticed her friend's reaction whenever he came into the ward. And, as Sir Leonard Wylie's right-hand man, he was a frequent visitor to the ward that contained a number of patients with chest complaints.

'I'm glad to hear it,' she said warmly and without an axe of her own to grind. She was unmoved by the looks and the magnetism that seemed to sweep so many girls off their feet. 'He may be just as nice as you seem to think and I won't deny that he has charm. But he knows just how to use it to his own ends, Daisy. I think everyone would be sorry to see your name added to his long list of conquests. You take things so much to heart, you know.' She smiled warmly. 'Take my advice and steer clear of him.'

Daisy was a dreamer and that could be very dangerous, Patti felt. She might weave dreams about a man that totally ignored the obviously sensuality of his nature that no girl should trust. Romantic dreams that had no chance of coming true for Gavin Fletcher seemed to be a determined bachelor who took all that women offered him and gave little in return.

Patti had known a man very like him, but she had not allowed him to break her heart. She was made of sterner stuff than Daisy who was sensitive and very vulnerable and much too likely to tumble into love with a charming rake.

Trish King put her head around the door at that moment. 'Time to do the teas, girls. You'll have to come back to that later . . .'

'It's done,' Daisy said. 'We were just coming, Staff.'

She was astonished how angry she felt with Patti who was her friend and who cared enough to want to warn her against making a fool of herself over a womaniser. She was glad that the staff nurse had disturbed them before she flared up and said something to Patti that she would certainly have regretted.

'Oh, good . . . !' Trish beamed on them. 'It's lovely to have someone really reliable on the ward when Sister isn't on duty. Some girls think they can relax and waste time just because I'm not a dragon by nature.' She whisked away.

Patti looked rueful. 'I know,' she said wryly. 'I'm interfering and you hate me for it. So would I. There's nothing worse than well-meaning friends handing out unwanted advice. Anyway, it isn't necessary, is it? You're much too level-headed to get involved with the Gavin Fletchers of this world!'

As they went round with the teas, the thin slices of bread and butter, and the cake, fruit or madeira, that they knew perfectly well would find its way to the visitors in some cases, Daisy was still seething with resentment.

It was all very well to be commended for her level head, but it seemed to Daisy that level-headed girls missed out on a lot of fun! Why should she always be sensible and cautious—and stuck with dreary men who only wanted to use her as a sounding-board for their clever theories? Why shouldn't she go out with Gavin Fletcher and dice with danger like other girls? Why did everyone assume that he was so irresistible and so persuasive that she would fall into bed with him at the lift of a finger if they thought she was so level-headed? It was perfectly possible that he just wanted to be friendly and did not have any evil designs on her at all, surely?

It was perfectly possible that he would never ask her again, she told herself stringently. If she really wanted to dice with danger then she'd better present herself at the Kingfisher that evening in her prettiest dress!

He would not be there, of course. She knew it with a sinking of her heart. He was not to be taken seriously at the best of times, she suspected—and she had said no! Why did she suppose that he would be in the pub in the hope that she would change her mind?

Anyway, she was going to the cinema that evening. She had arranged it with Joanne that morning. For once, Joanne did not have a date with one or other of the many men in her life.

The film was a love story with an unhappy ending, highly-praised by the critics for its very sensitive handling of an emotive subject, and Daisy was looking forward to a good cry. She liked a romantic story and one did get fed up at times with the predictably happy ending. It seemed to Daisy that they were few and far between in real life. Not many romances survived the hothouse atmosphere of a hospital, for instance, and Hartlake too often lived up to its wry nickname of Heartache Hospital . . .

Joanne was in the bath. The heady scent of bath salts permeated the tiny flat when Daisy let herself into it and she was instantly suspicious.

She opened the bathroom door and spoke through a cloud of steam. 'Hi! I'm home!' A slender arm emerged from the bubbles to wave. Joanne was luxuriating at full length in the perfumed water that reached up to her chin. 'I can't smell anything cooking,' Daisy went on cautiously. 'Are we eating out, after all?' It was Joanne's turn to organise the evening meal.

'Daisy! I didn't give it a thought! I *am* sorry!' Truly contrite, Joanne sat up swiftly, water streaming from her breasts and the glorious chestnut hair clinging damply in tight curls about her lovely face.

'Something else on your mind,' Daisy said in affectionate and understanding resignation, mentally waving goodbye to their visit to the cinema. She knew her Joanne.

'The most gorgeous man! A dream! He's taking me to dine and dance at the Caprice! Such a change from doctors or med students without two pennies to rub together,' she declared with feeling. 'I couldn't say no to that kind of offer, could I?'

'Who could?' Daisy passed the thick towel for which Joanne was groping rather wildly. 'Where did you meet this dream?'

'Oh, he's a patient. Was, rather. Discharged today, in fact. He's been coming for physio after a rather nasty car accident that's left him with a slight limp. I told him to continue with the exercises and he said that dancing was one of the best exercises he knew and would I like to do it with him.' She wrapped the towel about her slim body and stepped out of the bath. 'Are you starving? I feel dreadful,' she said penitently.

'Don't worry. I'll run down for some fish and chips,' Daisy said lightly. 'But first I must have some tea. Do you want a cup?'

'Please . . .'

Daisy went to the kitchen and switched on the kettle and got out the cups. Joanne vanished into the bedroom only to reappear seconds later with a stricken face. 'Gosh, Daisy, I'd completely forgotten. That film at the Odeon!'

Daisy smiled at her warmly. 'It doesn't matter. There's always another evening.'

'Are you sure? I expect I could leave a message at the Caprice for Michael . . .'

'Don't be daft! Give up an evening with a gorgeous man to sit in the pictures with me! I wouldn't let you do it,' Daisy said firmly. She hesitated and then swept on: 'Anyway, I'd forgotten the film, too. I've arranged to meet someone.'

Joanne was relieved. 'That's all right, then. Anyone I know?'

'I don't think so.' Daisy could not be sure. It did seem unlikely that someone like Gavin Fletcher could have overlooked a girl as strikingly beautiful and as popular with his sex as Joanne.

'Not Richard, then?'

'Not Richard,' she agreed.

Joanne got the message. She moved towards the door. 'Well, I hope he's as good-looking as mine,' she said and went away to dress.

Having made the tea, Daisy waited a moment or two before pouring it into the cups . . . and, as so often, slipped idly into a dream . . .

Herself and Gavin, dining and dancing at the Caprice, most romantic of nightclubs and haunt of the famous and wealthy. Looking lovely in a dream of a dress and Gavin looking down at her, as she danced in his arms, with a certain glow in his dark eyes that meant so much more than sexual appraisal and intent. Whirling into a blissful, magical world where nothing mattered but the love they felt for each other. That look in his eyes could only mean one thing. At any moment, his arms would tighten about her and he would rest his cheek against her hair and softly murmur in her ear . . .

'Did you make the tea, Daisy?'

Jerked back to reality, she gave a little sigh. Dreams were all very well, but some were never likely to come true. A girl only had to look at Gavin Fletcher to know that he was not the marrying kind, she thought wistfully.

She took tea into Joanne who sat at the small dressing-table, brushing her lovely hair and coaxing it into soft curls.

Joanne was quite beautiful.

Daisy had heard herself described as a pretty girl often enough and her mirror told her that vivid blue eyes in an oval face, the delicately fair skin that went with ash-blonde hair and a rather sweet mouth that was swift to smile added up to a certain prettiness. But Joanne was beautiful with her cascading chestnut curls and wide grey eyes and the lovely peaches and cream complexion and the golden smile that held every man spellbound. More than anything, she did not seem to know that she was beautiful . . . and that was endearing.

Being a cool blonde had its disadvantages, Daisy often felt, envying that rich, warm beauty that captivated the men in a moment. Joanne looked as though she might melt into a man's arms . . . and so she did, very often, for she was impulsive and warm-hearted and she fell in and out of love as though it was a very enjoyable game. At the same time, no one could accuse her of being without heart or morals.

Daisy was shy and she took life and love rather more seriously than her friends. As a result, most men seemed to think that she was reserved or cold or just not interested . . . or was it only that they just didn't notice her when Joanne was around? Daisy had resigned herself to living in Joanne's shadow to some extent and did not really mind that most men only sought her out to talk about her beautiful friend or to expound their theories.

But Gavin Fletcher was different. He was the kind of man that Joanne drew like a magnet—and the kind that Daisy seldom seemed to attract! So she was very tempted to take him up on that unexpected invitation, after all.

It was not much of a commitment to meet a man for a drink, she told herself. And perhaps it was a heaven-sent opportunity to find out for herself if he was as nice as she hoped, or if it was time to stop indulging in foolish dreams about someone who was really as black as grapevine rumours painted him!

The flat was very quiet and suddenly lonely when Joanne went out in a flurry of excitement to meet her date. Daisy tidied the small flat with her usual good-natured acceptance of Joanne's inability to dress for a special occasion without leaving almost the entire contents of her wardrobe scattered about the place. She had finally decided on a sophisticated and very sexy black frock that enhanced her rich colouring and warm beauty and provocative figure and Daisy did not doubt that her friend would come home in the early hours bubbling over with news of her latest conquest. It seemed that no man could resist Joanne when she had made up her mind to a light-hearted love affair. No doubt this one would be as short-lived as all the others, for Joanne's heart was as fickle as it was impulsive.

Daisy continued to be torn between temptation and hesitation. But ten to eight found her walking at a fairly brisk pace along the shabby turning that led to the High Street and the hospital and the Kingfisher. She was still in two minds. If she eventually decided not to enter the pub she meant to buy herself some fish and chips and return to the flat and curl up to watch television for the rest of the evening.

Still in uniform, she had wrapped her cloak about her against a slight drizzle of rain. Her only concession to a possible meeting with Gavin Fletcher was the unbraiding of her thick plaits. Her long, pale hair rippled in silky waves from a centre parting and shining wings of hair fell about her pretty face.

As she pushed her way through the swing door of the pub, her heart beating hard with shyness and a little excitement and a great deal of nervousness, the lights of the bar set up a sparkle among the raindrops in her hair.

Daisy did not like pubs. She did not think that she had ever walked into one on her own before and she was sure that everyone in the place was staring at her with curiosity or an offensive kind of speculation. It was filled to capacity and the noise was overwhelming.

She stood uncertainly in the crowd, scanning faces and hoping that Gavin Fletcher would come forward to claim her. There did not seem to be any sign of him. About to turn away, disappointed and knowing it was stupid to expect him to be there when she had not agreed to meet him, she suddenly caught sight of him—and her heart plummeted.

His dark head was very close to a bright blonde one and Daisy did not mistake the intimacy in the way he placed a hand on the girl's knee and leaned to speak directly into her ear. The girl laughed and sent him a sparkling, mock-reproachful glance that was full of flirtatious come-on and then she moved a little closer to him on the padded seat.

Daisy found her way to the door, rather blindly. What had she expected? Everyone knew what he was! He had only been chatting her up, trying it on as he did with so many of the nurses. When she had not responded like that rather brassy blonde, he had instantly forgotten her. He was not just a flirt. She could forgive that. He was a rake with only one thing in mind where any girl was concerned!

She almost had to fight her way out of the pub for a crowd of medical students in high spirits were forcing their way in . . . and their cheers and shouts and good-natured jostling of each other attracted attention. Gavin looked across at them and saw the girl with the long, pale hair and legs that he instantly recognised beneath the blue check skirt of her uniform frock. He leaped to his feet.

Daisy paused on the pavement outside the pub, fighting tears. She felt that he had deliberately humiliated her, quite forgetting that he had probably not expected her to turn up at the pub. How could he make up to that girl whose bright colouring so obviously came out of a bottle and whose instant reaction to his overtures did not say much for her morals? How could he let her stand there, lost and self-conscious and the target for any man who thought she was looking for someone to buy her a drink, while he openly proved his preference for the kind of girl who was not likely to say no to any of his suggestions?

Gavin thrust open the door and looked out, a frown in his dark eyes. He felt instant relief as he saw her, his suspicions confirmed. It *was* Daisy! He had been slightly thrown by the long hair that he did not remember.

'Daisy!' She did not turn or glance his way. He caught

her arm as she was on the point of hurrying away. 'Looking for me?' he asked lightly.

She pulled her arm from his hand. 'No.'

Gavin looked down at her. It was early summer and the lightness of the evening enabled him to see the stony expression in her blue eyes. He also saw that they were swimming with tears. 'What's the matter?' he asked gently. 'Some idiot stood you up?'

She wanted to point out that he was the idiot, but honesty compelled her to admit that she was the biggest fool for believing that he had meant that casual invitation. She shook her head, chin tilting with a hint of pride. 'No.' She turned away, began to walk along the pavement.

Gavin fell into step beside her. She was very pretty and rather sweet and he did not like to see a girl in tears. 'Come and have a drink, Daisy. It'll cheer you up.'

'No,' she said, very firm.

'That seems to be your favourite word,' he said, amused. 'I wonder if I can coax you into saying something a little more encouraging . . . like maybe!' His eyes twinkled.

Daisy paused. 'Please go back to your friends.' She was hurt and dismayed that he could be so light of heart and so uncaring after the way he had treated her.

'I'd rather be with you,' Gavin said lightly—and found that he meant it. There was something rather appealing about this slender girl with her pale hair and rather tremulous mouth and her prickly pride . . .

CHAPTER THREE

DAISY almost stamped her foot.

She was annoyed by his persistence. It was rather too
late for him to try to make amends, she thought crossly.
If he had really wanted her company he would have been
waiting for her, looking out for her, hurrying to greet her
and take care of her . . . but he had ignored her and
deliberately put his hand on that girl's knee to show the
world that they were on intimate terms!

She did not know why he had followed her from the
pub and was now refusing to take no for an answer. But
she was not appeased and far from flattered. And she
was furious with herself for weakly giving in to temptation and coming to meet him when he had not cared a
snap of his fingers if she turned up or not. There was
always another girl for a man like Gavin Fletcher!

'I'm going home,' she said stiffly.

'The Nunnery?' he asked, smiling, using the Hartlake
nickname for the Nurses' Home. Part of the sprawling
complex of hospital buildings, it was presided over by a
motherly Home Sister and contained a number of bed-
sitters and small flats that could be shared by two, three
or four girls.

Sister Vernon often closed her eyes to minor breaches
of the rules by "her girls", but could be moved to cold
and implacable fury if anyone took blatant advantage of
her kind heart and gentle nature.

For the first year of training, Daisy had lived in, sharing a flat with three other girls in her set. But as soon as she began her second year she had applied for Matron's permission to live out and moved into the tiny flat with Joanne. The young instinctively chafe at rules and regulations and many girls went into nursing with a view to escaping parental authority and vigilance. Home Sister, sweetie though she was, was still something of a substitute parent and her kindly eye could be all-seeing.

Daisy had been happy enough at The Nunnery, but she felt more mature and independent since she had left its shelter. There was rent and other bills to be paid and she shared expenses with Joanne. There was food to be bought and cooked, the flat to be kept clean, washing and ironing to be done and it was true that she did not always feel like bothering after a long day on the ward. But Joanne did her share—and it was fun to live with someone as lively as Joanne who was very apt to throw a party on the spur of the moment.

The other flats were occupied by Hartlake staff and the alternation of night and day duties meant that there was always someone about willing to make tea, to talk shop, to exchange grapevine gossip. It was an extension of the Nurses' Home, perhaps . . . but Daisy liked the freedom to come and go as she pleased.

'The Nunnery?' Gavin repeated.

Daisy shook her head. 'No.'

'You don't live in?'

'Not now.'

She did not mean to be forthcoming, he thought wryly. Did she dislike him so much—or was it only that she was momentarily off men because one had let her down? 'Do you live at home then?' he persisted.

Daisy sighed. 'No. I share a flat with a girl-friend,' she said, rather reluctantly, but with an inbred gentleness of nature that did not allow her to be blatantly rude to someone that she did not know very well.

She thought she saw a swift gleam of satisfaction in his dark eyes and wished that she had been rude. He need not think that a flat of her own provided him with *carte blanche* for the kind of activities that could never take place in the Nurses' Home . . . hence its nickname!

'If it's within walking distance, I'll walk with you,' he declared lightly, confidently. 'Otherwise, I'll drive you. My car is parked in Clifton Street.'

'I don't want you to bother,' Daisy said coldly.

'But I want to bother,' he said in a voice that suddenly did not allow for argument. 'Now, which is it? Walk – or car?'

Daisy bit her lip. But she was not the first woman to succumb to that masterful note in his voice. 'I live in Clifton Street,' she admitted.

'Convenient!' He smiled down at her. 'Come on, girl . . . you're getting wet!' He took her arm and began to hurry her along the pavement. The rain had suddenly decided to turn heavy.

Again, Daisy pulled from his touch. It disturbed her just a little. She drew her cloak more tightly about herself, glancing at him. The rain was steadily damping the light-coloured raincoat he had shrugged into while they talked to protect his formal dark suit and it was causing the dark hair to tighten into curls on the nape of his neck. Sensing her glance, he turned his head, smiled. Daisy refused to smile back.

She was grateful that it was such a short distance to the house. Resolutely he plied her with questions about her work on Fleming, her opinion of Sister Sweet, how she got on with the other nurses, the friend she shared a flat with, her home town, her family ... and Daisy answered him in flat, rather unfriendly monosyllables.

She had made up her mind to dislike him. But that did not seem to bother the heart that stirred at his touch and leaped at his smile and stored up every meaningless word for later. He was more attractive than any man had the right to be and those sensual good looks, that disarming smile and that pleasant voice seemed to be playing havoc with her good sense.

She wondered again why he had followed her from the pub and insisted on walking her home. She did not believe that he was at all attracted. She was not really his type, Daisy thought wryly, remembering the girl whose blonde good looks and easy manners and encouraging response was not at all like her own.

He was being kind. Heaven knew why! He did not even know her—and it had nothing to do with conscience for he had obviously forgotten that earlier suggestion that they should meet. He thought she had gone to the Kingfisher to meet someone else and been let down ... and he was sorry for her!

It was humiliating. Daisy wished she knew how to convince him that she did not want his compassion or his company. She had no experience of men like Gavin Fletcher who did not seem to know when they were not wanted.

'This is it,' she said abruptly, stopping, searching for her key in the purse she took from her pocket. 'Good-night.'

Gavin mounted the stone steps in a couple of strides and proceeded to study the bell-pushes and nameplates.

'Miss D. Palmer . . . Miss J. Laidlaw,' he read. 'That's your friend?'

'Yes.'

'Nice girl, is she?'

'Yes.' Daisy hesitated with her key in her hand, wondering how on earth she could get rid of this persistent man who seemed oblivious to hints.

'I'd like to meet her.'

'She's out,' Daisy said quickly . . . and then could have kicked herself for that impulsive answer. She suspected that his probing had been entirely to the purpose of finding out if the flat was empty. Or was it a ridiculous conceit on her part to imagine that he might have designs on her just because he had insisted on walking home with her?

'Another time, then,' he said carelessly, as though it was a foregone conclusion that he would become a part of her life in one way or another in the future. 'What's her first name?' he added, standing with his back to the heavy front door, blocking her access to the lock.

'Joanne.' She wondered why he was trying to keep her talking.

'Joanne Laidlaw. I think I've heard it. A nurse, is she?'

'She's training in physiotherapy.' Daisy tried to brush past him. 'Excuse me. I want to open the door . . .'

Gavin took the key from her hand, slipped it into the lock and pushed open the heavy door to reveal the hallway and a number of closed doors and a staircase that led to more of the tiny flats that were replicas of the one she shared with Joanne. 'Which floor?'

'You're not coming up!' she said, rather too quickly—and saw a smile flicker in the dark eyes. He was laughing at her, she thought with a sudden heaviness of heart. She knew she had sounded about thirteen and terrified! He must think that she had never had anything to do with men, she thought bitterly. She was not very experienced, it was true. But it was galling that Gavin Fletcher should realise it. It was even more galling that he probably did not really mean to take advantage of the fact. It was all just a game to him!

'Just as you say,' he said carelessly.

Daisy was absurdly disappointed. 'My key,' she said, holding out her hand.

He dangled it provocatively, eyes dancing. 'A kiss for it.'

She froze. 'Go to hell!' she said, meaning it.

Gavin looked down at the small, angry face and was unexpectedly stirred by its appealing prettiness. 'I wondered when you would force yourself to be rude to me,' he said gently. 'You wanted to be rid of me outside the pub, didn't you? Any other girl would have told me to go to hell long before, you know. But I imagine that you find it very difficult to say no to anyone, Daisy.'

She was very angry, trembling. She was very sure of his meaning and she was shocked, resentful and quite furious at the slur on her morals.

'You're wrong,' she said fiercely, snatching her key from his hand. 'I never say yes!'

Gavin said quickly: 'That isn't what I meant and I'm sure that you don't! *Virgin* is written all over you. But perhaps you've never been tempted,' he added, smiling. 'You'll say yes one day, you know.'

'Not to you!'

'I can be very persuasive,' he drawled and, before she knew what he was about, he took her head in both his hands, sliding his strong fingers into the silky mass of her hair, and kissèd her lightly on the lips.

Daisy thrust him away, but her whole body had quivered in eager and delicious and rather alarming response to that light and utterly meaningless kiss. She glared at him. 'Will you get out of here?' she demanded, seething.

He was tall and impressive—and damnably sure of himself as he stood in the shabby hall, looking down at her with that half-smile lurking about his sensual mouth. Daisy hated him, knowing that he was probably aware of that instinctive response in her to the touch of his lips. He was a man who knew all the potency of his physical magnetism, she thought bitterly.

She wished it was possible to push him out of the house and close the front door firmly in his face. But she knew she lacked the strength and she did not mean to indulge in the indignity of struggling with him.

'I can't say I'm sorry, you know,' Gavin said with truth. Her lips had been surprisingly sweet and the soft perfume of her hair had stirred his senses just a little. He had kissed her to tease, rather amused by her defensive distrust of him. But he found himself wanting rather badly to kiss her again. 'I enjoyed it,' he added softly. 'Didn't you?'

He was outrageous! Daisy bridled. 'No.'

'Then I'm losing my touch,' he said with that disarming smile.

Daisy refused to be disarmed. 'I've heard too much about your touch,' she said coldly.

'My reputation is before me,' he said, wry. 'I won't deny any of it. Obviously, you wouldn't believe me.'

'No,' she said flatly.

Gavin was suddenly and strangely determined that one day this girl would say *yes, yes, yes* and move willingly into his arms and lift that pretty face for his kiss with all the eagerness that a man could wish. One day . . .

For the moment, she did not trust him at all and she did not want to like him. He was intrigued. Too many girls had responded too readily. It had suited him well enough in the past. But suddenly he felt that there would be a great deal of delight in coaxing this reluctant girl into his arms. She was pretty and she had spirit for all her shyness and obvious inexperience.

Daisy walked towards the stairs. She did not think he would have the effrontery to follow her. She sensed his gaze on her very straight back as she went up the rather narrow staircase with its worn linoleum covering and neglected paintwork. She was much too conscious of her slight but quite attractive figure, the sway of her hips that she really could not help and the slenderness of legs that she knew were worthy of a second glance from any man. She was not in the least bit flattered by the way he stood watching her with a little glow of admiration in his dark eyes. She did not need to turn, to look at him, to know just *how* he looked. He was quite blatant in his sensual pursuit of a woman.

Daisy was astonished that he was in pursuit of her. But it could only be a very fleeting fancy and if she did not encourage him at all then he would soon find another girl to play his light-hearted game of loving that was not loving at all!

Gavin heard the sharp snap of her flat door with its obvious finality. He had not expected her to turn, to smile, to relent and ask him up for a drink or a cup of coffee. She was not that kind of girl. Warm and friendly to her friends, she would give short shrift to a near-stranger that she did not trust . . . in her gentle, much-too polite way that hesitated to hurt or offend, he thought wryly. He hoped she would never run into the kind of man who supposed that shy gentleness and reluctance to snub sprang from a desire to encourage. Somehow, he knew and understood her. Another man might have been misled, encouraged . . . and turned nasty with frustration and disappointment when he discovered that she was really not interested.

Even though he had kissed her. He did not regret it, but he was sorry that he had alarmed her. She had concealed it well but she had been frightened. Yet he had carefully kept all hint of that stirring passion from his kiss. He reminded himself that Daisy did not know him except as a doctor she occasionally saw about the hospital . . . and his reputation was pretty black. It had never bothered him unduly. Now he wondered if it would always keep the shy and inexperienced and easily alarmed Daisy from liking him, trusting him. He wondered what it was about this particular girl that made him so concerned to win her liking and trust.

There were plenty of women in the world and he had found most of them willing, he reminded himself as he strode through the rain to his parked car. Why on earth should he bother his head about an oddly-named junior nurse with little to recommend her but a pretty face and a lovely pair of legs and a tendency to say *no* much too often?

Daisy closed the door of the flat and stood with her back firmly against it, still trembling. She waited for several minutes, half-expecting his knock, his voice with that hint of command in it. She was afraid she might open the door at his request . . . and told herself that she would not want to attract the attention of her neighbours or create the kind of scene that would bring them crowding out in curiosity.

There was nothing. No knock, no voice. Daisy moved away from the door, casting her cloak over a chair, a tiny sigh escaping her. He should not have kissed her and she would not forgive him for it. But it had been rather nice . . . disturbing, but nice.

She could still feel his strong hands twined in her hair. Her scalp tingled with the memory of his touch. She could still feel the slight pressure of his rather sensual mouth on her own. Her body tingled with the memory of excitement.

He was too attractive, too exciting. He was dangerous. She must make sure that they were never alone again. She must make sure that she never encouraged him to believe that she liked him, wanted him . . .

She pulled up her thoughts with a little jerk of dismay. She certainly did not want him. She had no intention of liking him. She had indulged in silly dreams about a man she did not know just because he was good-looking and wore a white coat. Daisy and the doctor, she jeered, mocking herself. From her earliest teens, she had dreamed of marrying a doctor and perhaps she had become a nurse in the hope of fulfilling that dream rather than because she really wanted to care for the sick and disabled.

There were plenty of doctors at Hartlake. Richard would qualify very shortly. Why didn't she dream about him or one of the others instead of wasting romantic thoughts on a rake like Gavin Fletcher?

Romance and Gavin Fletcher just did not go together. To Daisy's mind, romance meant real and lasting love and loving was synonymous with marriage. No one could suppose that a man like Gavin Fletcher was capable of real and lasting love for any woman, and not one of the many grapevine rumours about him had ever hinted at an inclination towards marriage. It was madness to think of loving him, Daisy told herself firmly . . . and wondered with a little surprise how she had reached *loving* in her thoughts when she had already discarded liking and wanting and trusting where Gavin Fletcher was concerned . . .

It was very much later that Daisy suddenly remembered that she was hungry. Apart from a cup of tea with Joanne, she had not had anything since lunch. She had meant to get herself some fish and chips and it would have been much more practical and a lot less disturbing if she had done just that instead of weakly going to meet a man who had forgotten that he had ever wanted to meet her!

Without appetite, she made herself a sandwich and a cup of hot chocolate. She tried to read, but her thoughts skated off the page. She tried to watch television, but the choice between sport or politics or an off-beat play was no choice at all to Daisy.

In the end, she went early to bed and lay in a tight little huddle trying to sleep, trying to rub a very vivid picture of a man's good-looking face from the slate of her mind, trying to feel nothing but dislike and contempt for a man she would certainly see again much too soon . . .

Her nerves were at full stretch by the time he walked into the ward in the wake of Sir Leonard. Daisy had been trying not to think about him ever since she came on duty, rather heavy-eyed. She had failed. It was all very well to tell herself firmly that a good nurse thought of nothing but the care and welfare of her patients when she was on the ward, never allowing the personal to intrude into her professional life.

She could not have been thinking of her patient when she neglected to leave the still-needed oxygen mask within easy reach of Mr Paine who had been very ill with broncho-pneumonia and spent some time in an oxygen tent, needing special nursing. An oxygen cylinder now stood beside his bed for occasional use.

Mr Paine was almost well again, but there were moments of breathing difficulty that was due rather more to anxiety than respiratory problems. He liked the reassurance of knowing that he had only to stretch out his hand to the mask to gain instant relief. That morning, Daisy had tidied his bed and locker in readiness for Sir Leonard Wylie's round and left him. Some time later, he had wanted the mask—and he had been quite distressed by the time he had managed to attract the attention of a passing nurse.

Sister Sweet had been very cross with the penitent Daisy.

Nor could she have been thinking of her patient when she absent-mindedly offered a feeding-cup to poor old Mr Lane whose terribly arthritic and painfully deformed hands were, like the rest of him, virtually useless. A chronic case of rheumatoid arthritis, he was admitted from time to time for rest for his inflamed joints, a course of anti-inflammatory drugs and a high protein diet. He was a dear old man, a favourite with the nurses, and it was typical of him that he should attempt to take the cup to please her. Inevitably, the entire contents had spilled over him and the bed. That had meant putting him into clean pyjamas and changing the sheets and as every movement caused him a great deal of pain, Daisy was thoroughly chastened by the time the task was finished.

Sister Sweet threatened to send her to Matron. Instead, she sent her into the sluice to help Patti who was washing and sterilising bedpans. As it was really a job for a very junior nurse, Daisy felt like a naughty schoolgirl sent to stand in the corner. She was quite convinced that she was not and never would be a good nurse.

'Never mind,' Patti sympathised. 'We all have our off days.'

'Oh, don't!' Daisy wailed, near to tears. 'I don't deserve anyone to be nice to me! That poor man—and it was all my fault. He suffers so dreadfully and you know it's agony when we have to make his bed and all he does is apologise for being such a nuisance! He was determined to take the blame and said such nice things about me to Sister . . . and I hate myself!'

'I know the feeling,' Patti said. She reached for a box of tissues. 'Here! I suppose you haven't got a hanky!'

Daisy shook her head and fumbled for a tissue. She blew her nose, pulled herself together. 'It's being a beastly day,' she said bitterly.

'Something nice is just about to happen,' Patti said with a meaningful little twinkle in her eye. 'It's time for Sir Leonard's round. You might get a nice smile from Dr Fletcher if you play your cards right!' She was surprised when Daisy gave a short, rather contemptuous sniff and stalked from the sluice with her head high. Wondering, Patti continued cheerfully with one of the least popular chores of a nurse's day.

When Sir Leonard's round started, Daisy was in a side

ward with Staff Nurse Trish King, attending to a very overweight patient who had just been moved from the Cardiac Unit where he had been admitted after a minor heart attack. As was usual in such cases, he was extremely anxious about himself and very reluctant to make the least effort for fear that the agonising pain in his chest would return. He was making good progress, but it would take a few weeks for the nursing staff to reassure him and encourage him back to a normal way of life. In the meantime, it took two nurses to get the big man in and out of bed.

Daisy was relieved that she was not on the main ward when Gavin Fletcher walked into it. She had no desire to see him, she told herself sternly—although she knew very well that he would be blind and deaf to her existence during rounds, anyway.

Patti looked into the room. 'Well, you're a dark horse, I must say,' she accused Daisy, eyes dancing.

Daisy stared. 'What do you mean?'

'You obviously know Gavin Fletcher better than you've allowed your friends to believe,' Patti said, teasing. As Daisy still looked puzzled, she swept on: 'Anyway, he's paid you a remarkable compliment!'

'I don't know what you're talking about,' Daisy said firmly, plumping pillows. Trish King looked from one girl to the other with slightly amused curiosity.

'Go and see!' Patti gave her a little push towards the door and thrust a folder into her hand. 'Here! This is your excuse! It's Mr Carroll's X-rays and Sir Leonard is waiting for them.'

There was so much merriment in her friend's manner that Daisy was quite bewildered—and highly curious. Just a little reluctant, she went into the ward and walked to the bed where Sir Leonard, his Senior Registrar and a group of students were gathered with Sister Sweet.

Carefully not looking at anyone else, she handed the folder to Sister and stood, hands demurely behind her back, awaiting instructions. Sister sent her away and as she turned, glancing despite all her good intentions at Gavin Fletcher, she suddenly saw the little knot of daisies that he was sporting in the lapel of his white coat.

CHAPTER FOUR

THE colour surged into her small face.

Then she was very, very angry. How *dared* he do such a thing! It was blatant encouragement of totally unfounded gossip. Daisies in his lapel, indeed! It would be all over the hospital within the hour—and everyone would think just what Patti had thought and what she was no doubt gleefully explaining to Staff Nurse King at that very moment.

Because of her very unusual name, Daisy had attracted rather more notice than the average student nurse when she first came to Hartlake. Even now, many of the staff knew Daisy Palmer by name, if not by sight. No one would fail to link that name with the daisies that Gavin Fletcher had chosen to wear on his white coat for rounds that morning!

Daisy left the ward as quickly as she could with murder in her heart. She shut herself into the linen cupboard to cope with the fury that was threatening to burst its bounds. She did not know how she was going to punish Gavin Fletcher, but she would—somehow!

She hated him. He was despicable. He had deliberately set out to link their names—and everyone would believe that there was some kind of a relationship between them. And where Gavin Fletcher was concerned that did not do a girl's reputation any good at all!

Oh, it was too bad of him—and entirely without reason! The whole of Hartlake would be talking about

her and she was in quite enough trouble with Sister
Sweet just now without silly rumours to make it worse.
Sister Sweet frowned on the least hint of flirtation
between one of her nurses and a patient or a member of
the medical staff. She had been known to send Matron a
particularly bad report on a junior nurse's work just
because the girl had been caught in the kitchen with a
young patient's arm about her waist.

But where on earth had he found daisies, of all things?
Everyone knew that they died almost as soon as they
were picked! Then she thought of the hospital garden
that was such an unexpected and rather pleasant centre-
piece for the tall buildings. It was presided over by the
stone statue of the benevolent philanthropist, Sir Henry
Hartlake, who had founded the hospital, and its paved
paths were used as short cuts from one wing to the other
by a great many people.

Daisy remembered how she and the others of her set
had sat on the lawn in the bright sunshine of early
summer, talking and laughing and occasionally remembering to study. She remembered the daisies, too
. . . myriads of them on the lawn. The girls had made
daisy chains of them like the children that many of them
still were at heart in those days before work on the wards
gave them a new maturity.

Now it was again summer and the daisies sprinkled the
lawns—and Gavin Fletcher had probably walked
through the garden on his way to Fleming and the first of
Sir Leonard's rounds. No doubt it had appealed to his
sense of humour to bend down and pick a handful of
daisies and thrust them into his lapel just to tease and
infuriate her—and give the grapevine something to delight it! She could believe that it was typical of him!

Quivering, Daisy battled with her humiliation. She was hurt, too . . . in an odd kind of way. For it seemed that Gavin Fletcher could not have any real liking for her to expose her to speculation of the worst kind in such fashion.

Patti opened the door, looked in. 'There you are!' she announced, relieved. 'Sister sent me to find you . . . I think she wants you to do the medicine round with her.' She looked at Daisy's set face and came in, closing the door of the little room. 'Are you all right, Daisy?'

'Yes, of course.' Keeping her back to Patti, she busied herself unnecessarily with tidying a stack of sheets, newly returned from the laundry. Sister Sweet did not allow the linen cupboard to be untidy at any time.

'*Now*, Daisy,' Patti urged gently. 'Sister's on the warpath this morning. Don't keep her waiting.'

Daisy sighed. 'Why does she want *me*? I suppose I shall have to endure a lecture on the folly of flirting with senior doctors while I'm handing out tablets and coaxing reluctant patients to drink their nasty medicine.'

Patti grinned. '*Have* you been flirting with senior doctors? A tall, dark and handsome Registrar, for instance . . .?'

'No, I haven't!' Daisy snapped, unusually tart.

'Ouch!' Her friend's tone was rueful.

'Sorry,' Daisy said, instantly penitent. 'I didn't mean to bite your head off.'

'Sister will have *your* head on a trolley and served up to Matron if you don't get back to the ward in ten seconds,' Patti warned.

'Do you know, I don't think I care,' Daisy returned, rather bitterly. But she straightened her cap and hurried. She had felt the rough edge of Sister Sweet's tongue twice already and she suspected that she was about to get another helping . . .

Sister Sweet was very sour-faced when Daisy saw her at the drugs trolley, key at the ready. She could not begin the round without her for it was a very strict rule that there must always be two people to give out medicine or drugs, one to dispense the dosage and the other to check it carefully before it was given to the patient. It eliminated the risk of error.

Daisy enjoyed the round for it was a welcome breathing-space in the busy day. She always had a smile and a friendly word for each patient and it pleased her to see how they responded. Few grumbled, she found. Most of the men, however ill, managed a smile or some reply.

She liked working on a male ward although every nurse, pretty or not, had to run the gauntlet of meaningful looks or comments at times. She grew used to it very quickly and soon learned to cope with the cheekiest. It was a sure sign of recovery when a man began to notice the nurses who looked after him—and Patti had been known to declare in her usual blunt fashion that as soon as a man turned randy she knew he must be due for an early discharge from hospital.

Sister Sweet liked to take her time over the round when possible. It gave her an opportunity to talk to the patients and find out if they had any particular fear or problem. It also gave her an opportunity to assess their progress or decline with her experienced eye. She had been in charge of the ward for over a year and she was an excellent nurse, although she was not too popular with staff or patients.

She took her work very seriously indeed and it

annoyed her that some of the girls who came to Hartlake to train seemed to look upon nursing as just another job and resented the discipline and the routine of ward work. Dedicated herself, Sarah Sweet believed that nursing was a vocation and that any follower in Florence Nightingale's footsteps should embrace the long hours, the never-ending rounds and the hard work with real enthusiasm. She had no time for any nurse on her ward who was not prepared to work until she dropped if necessary.

She was unconsciously bidding to become as much of a legend as Sister Booth, her predecessor, who was still remembered for her rigid discipline and sharp tongue. Sister Booth had run the ward for many years with a rod of iron and reduced many of her nurses to tears and even awed consultants. Disliked by her colleagues, she had been much loved by the patients who very often got better against all odds just to please her . . . or so legend had it!

Sister Booth had been all heart for all that crusty exterior. It was said that Sarah Sweet did not have a heart at all—and Daisy believed it as she hurried along the ward and apologised with a little trepidation for keeping her waiting.

'Where were you, Nurse Palmer?' The tone was icy. Anger sparked in eyes that might have been rather lovely if they had been allowed to smile more often.

'In the linen cupboard, Sister . . . tidying the linen.'

There was a brief, ominous silence. Then: 'Did I tell you to do that?'

'No, Sister. I just thought . . .'

Daisy was not given time to explain. 'What *did* I tell you to do?' Sister Sweet interrupted, very brusque.

Daisy bit her lip, racked her brain. 'I can't remember, Sister,' she finally admitted, very reluctantly.

'You were not listening.' Her mouth tightened. 'I said you were to take Mr Groves to the bathroom and supervise his bath. Why did I find him wandering in the corridor wearing nothing but a pyjama top?'

Mr Groves was an elderly patient with nephritis and he was often confused by the drugs that were so necessary in his illness. He needed to be watched very carefully since he had been allowed out of bed.

Daisy stifled a nervous giggle. She must not laugh, although she could not help recalling how Mr Groves had horrified a hospital visitor on her way to the ward with the library trolley. He had suddenly appeared around a corner as naked as the day he was born and unaware of it. Fortunately, Sister had been off duty. Daisy and Patti had hustled the protesting Mr Groves into a bathroom while another nurse explained things to the startled spinster. It had been a moment of light relief in their long and busy day.

'I'm very sorry, Sister,' Daisy said with just the hint of a quiver in her voice.

Sister Sweet looked at her coldly. 'I don't think I want you on my ward, Nurse Palmer,' she said sternly. 'You are lazy and inattentive and the patients are suffering as a result. Go off duty and report to Matron in the morning. I doubt if I shall have you back on Fleming.'

'Sister!' Daisy was appalled. She had worked really hard throughout the fourteen months of her training and she had never been sent off a ward for failing to do her work properly. It would be a very black mark against her, she knew . . . and it was so unfair!

'You may send Nurse Parkin to help me with the

medicine round and then leave the ward,' Sister said implacably.

'Please, Sister, I really am sorry,' Daisy said anxiously. 'I know I've done some silly things today, but I've had something on my mind. I promise I'll be more careful in future. Please don't send me off duty.'

Sister Sweet was not prepared to relent. She was very cross with this girl who had promised so well and let her down so badly. Sir Leonard had said some very scathing things about Mr Paine's condition. That business of the out-of-reach oxygen mask had caused a slight setback for the patient and Sir Leonard had not been at all pleased. Any criticism of her nurses reflected on her, of course—and she set great store on the consultant's opinion of the way the ward was run.

'I am waiting, Nurse,' she said coldly. 'The medicine round should have started five minutes ago. Please tell Nurse Parkin to come and help me on your way off the ward.'

Daisy turned away without another word, her heart swelling. Hateful woman! It was bad enough to send her off, but to do it in front of patients who were obviously straining their ears to hear the low exchange. She had never been so humiliated.

She found Patti in the kitchen and passed on the message and then rushed from the ward, not trusting herself to tell even her friend what had happened. She was much too near to tears.

Sent off the ward! Sent to Matron for a reprimand and a warning! Transferred to a new ward with a bad report from Sister Sweet to dog her next few weeks!

Daisy wished she had never thought of nursing as a career. She wished she had never come to Hartlake.

Most of all, she wished that she had never set eyes on Gavin Fletcher.

He was entirely to blame, she thought angrily, convinced that her senior's attitude had very little to do with her work or her behaviour on the ward. Sarah Sweet was merely furious that Sir Leonard's Senior Registrar should appear to be advertising his affair with one of her nurses—and Daisy was being punished for that more than anything else! It was so unfair when there was no affair and not even an understanding between her and Gavin Fletcher—not that anyone would believe her, she thought bitterly. Those wretched daisies would be assumed to tell their own story!

She was almost running when she collided with Gavin as he came out of a side ward, the patient's case history in his hand. 'Hey! Fire or haemorrhage, Nurse?' he demanded lightly, catching her by the arm to steady her. He smiled down at her with friendly warmth. He had been hoping for a private word and for once there was no one else about.

Daisy threw off his hand. 'Don't talk to me!' she stormed, pale with anger.

He raised an eyebrow. 'That's a lot of fury, girl,' he drawled. 'What's it all about?'

She glared at him. 'You and your daisies,' she said scathingly. Impulsively she snatched the straggle of fast-fading little flowers from his coat and threw them to the floor, stamping on them. She was much too angry to care what she said or did. 'I've been sent off the ward and I'm seeing Matron tomorrow—and it's all thanks to you! I hope that you're satisfied!'

A frown leaped to his dark eyes. 'I don't think I understand,' he said slowly.

'Oh, but *I* do!' she retorted, very bitter. 'You didn't get what you wanted and that annoyed you and so you thought you'd make me a laughing-stock!'

His eyes narrowed. He looked at the tumultuous little face, so pale and strained . . . and then down at the crushed and bedraggled flowers on the floor. 'Did that annoy you so much?' he asked quietly. 'I'm sorry, Daisy. I thought it might please you.' His tone was wry. It had been an absurd impulse, but it had seemed to suit the way he felt about this girl. He liked her. He wanted to know more of her. He had hoped the little cluster of wild flowers might bring a swift and appreciative smile to her lovely eyes and soften her attitude to him.

'*Please* me! To have everyone talking about us!'

'Are they? I didn't think of that,' he admitted ruefully, realising too late that he had given the gossips a great deal of ammunition without the slightest intention of doing so. No wonder she was so cross. He knew that while the junior nurses could be persuaded into friendship with him they were always wary of Matron's displeasure. A little smile hovered about his lips. 'We could give them something to talk about,' he suggested softly, eyes twinkling.

She slapped his face, hard. 'Don't ever speak to me again unless you have to!' she flared.

Gavin was suddenly angry, too. He caught her wrist. 'That's enough!' he said sharply, his cheek stinging from the blow. 'You must be mad to start a quarrel where half the hospital can hear!' He looked up and down the wide, still-empty corridor and then thrust the patient's folder at her. 'Here, take this!' he commanded.

Startled into obedience, Daisy did so. Now that he had a free hand, Gavin moved fast. He threw open the door of the linen cupboard and pulled her into the small room with him before she realised what he meant to do. He kicked the door shut and looked down at her with a little anger in his eyes. She was wary and stiff with fury—and he knew that he was hurting her with his grip on her wrist. She was a slight girl with an air of fragility that was conveyed by the fairness of hair and skin, the delicacy of small features and small bones.

'Now! If you've anything more to say get it off your chest. Then perhaps we can sort out this rather stupid misunderstanding,' he said grimly.

Daisy struggled to free herself. He was very strong and very determined and, she realised, extremely annoyed. Well, so was she! And with a great deal of justification! 'You're hurting me!' she said coldly.

'I ought to put you over my knee and spank you,' Gavin told her bluntly. 'You're behaving like a spoiled brat instead of a responsible adult.'

Daisy glowered. 'If you don't let me go, I shall start screaming,' she threatened. 'Just think what *that* will do for your reputation—and your career, Dr Fletcher!'

'Gavin shook his head, baffled. 'What did I do?' he marvelled. 'And what happened to *you*? How did you turn into a vixen overnight? I thought you were such a sweet little thing.'

She tried to wrench her wrist from his firm clasp. 'You thought I was an easy lay,' she corrected, icy. 'You thought you only had to smile and waft a bit of charm about as usual and I'd . . .'

He stopped her mouth with his own, hard and angry, forcing her back against the linen-laden shelves of the small room. She was so shocked that all the fight went out of her abruptly. He put his arms about her and a hint of passion crept into his kiss, the pressure of his lean body against her own. Daisy knew she should thrust him away. But there was a trembling weakness in her limbs and a quickening excitement in her veins and a feeling deep down in the secret places of her body that she had never known before. Her heart was beating very hard and very fast and her senses were swimming. Just when she thought she must be about to faint, he raised his head.

Gavin was shaken. He had not meant to kiss her. He had only wanted to silence her, disliking the kind of thing that temper was urging her to say. Certainly he had never meant to kiss her in just that way. He had come very near to losing control of the sensuality that was always a temptation and often a torment. He was a very passionate man and he had learned at an early age to keep a tight rein on the wanting that was swift to leap and insistent on its satisfaction. It was a rare woman who could catch him unawares. But Daisy had done it, he thought wryly.

Something in the sweetness of her lips, for all their reluctance, perhaps. Something in the faint perfume of her hair or the gentle, yielding softness of her slight body. Whatever it was, it had slipped beneath his guard, unleashed the hot desire and almost urged him past the point of no return.

He was shaken by the force of his feelings. He could not remember that any woman in the past had ever stirred him so powerfully. Women were just women, he had always felt . . . to be taken, enjoyed and kissed goodbye. He doubted that he could settle for spending the rest of his life with just one woman. There were too many exciting women in the world for a sensual, demanding man who had looks and charm and money in his favour.

He did not think that he was as black as most people liked to paint him. He seldom seduced virgins. He had never taken any woman against her will. He did not mouth empty words of love to persuade a woman into bed with him and he prided himself on bringing honesty and responsibility to a relationship. He had not set out to hurt anyone deliberately in his life. He was a good son to his parents, a good brother, a good friend . . . and he was a good lover who looked after the women in his life while they lasted.

Still holding her, he rested his cheek against the soft braids of her hair. The stiff little cap had fallen to the floor, unnoticed, along with the case history that had slipped from her nerveless fingers. 'I didn't mean that to happen,' he said quietly.

'It doesn't matter.' Daisy stood very still in that oddly comforting embrace, puzzled at the way the anger had drained out of her, a little frightened by the emotion that had taken its place, and wondering where they went from here.

'Feeling better?' Gavin drew away and looked down at her solemn little face. He knew an impulse to kiss her again—and resisted it, remembering where that first kiss had almost led him. He would have to be very careful in his dealings with this girl, who was different from any other he had known. It threatened to be a case of spontaneous combustion, he thought wryly—one touch of hands, of lips, of bodies and they both burst into flame. He knew just what a dangerous flame it could be when an innocent and utterly inexperienced girl was involved. He did not doubt that she was a virgin for all that eager and instinctive response.

Daisy looked at his cheek where the marks of her fingers still lingered, faint but in evidence. She had struck him in anger and now she marvelled. She had not known that she was capable of that murderous fury. And she had not known that she was capable of that tidal wave of wanting. It was all the more alarming because he was almost a stranger. She hoped he did not know what his kiss had evoked in her—but she was very sure that he did.

She pulled out of his arms, wondering how she came to be in them when she did not even like him. 'I shouldn't have flown at you like that,' she said, rather lamely. 'Even if you deserve it . . .'

'Tell me what it's all about.' He smiled at her encouragingly.

'Oh, not now. It doesn't seem to matter any more,' she declared, weary. She felt quite exhausted after all that emotion. 'I must go before Sister finds out that I haven't left the ward. If she'd walked in on us just now I should be leaving for good, I expect—sacked on the spot!' She sighed. 'It seems so ridiculous to be sent home to do nothing when there are never enough hands for all the work there is on the ward.'

'Why don't you try an apology?' Gavin said lightly. 'She may have calmed down by this time.'

'I did apologise. She didn't want to listen. People talk about Sister Booth and what a dragon she was! I reckon Sister Sweet knocks her into a cocked hat!' she said with feeling.

Gavin smiled. 'Oh, I don't know. She can be quite human when she lets her hair down.'

Daisy looked at him askance, fancying a hint of

reminiscence behind the words. 'Is there any nurse at Hartlake that you haven't seen with her hair down?' she demanded, slightly accusing.

He laughed, eyes dancing. 'I've been busy in the last few years, I admit. But not *that* busy!' He touched his hand to the thick braids that bound her small head. 'How about you, Daisy?' he asked softly, smiling. 'Are *you* going to let your hair down for me?'

It was impossible to mistake his meaning, the glow in the dark eyes. 'I'd be a fool if I did,' she retorted without hesitation. 'I don't mean to be just another name on the list for any man!' She bent to pick up her cap and the thick folder from the floor.

'Not even if I promise to put it up in lights?' he urged, teasing, warm.

He was too attractive. Daisy knew a little quiver of response to his charm. 'No,' she said firmly.

'Ten feet tall . . .?'

She would not smile at his coaxing tone, relent before the urging in his smile. 'No.'

He was suddenly serious. 'I guess it's just as well,' he said quietly. 'I love them and leave them and you're the type to get hurt. So I'll keep out of your life, I think . . .'

He took the folder and was gone, leaving Daisy with her head and her heart in a whirl of doubt and dismay and unmistakable disappointment.

CHAPTER FIVE

DAISY spent much of the afternoon in cleaning the flat, hoovering and dusting and polishing until everything gleamed. She had hoped that she wouldn't have time or energy over for thought or feeling, but it did not work out that way, after all.

Gavin Fletcher's handsome face kept coming between her and the job in hand. Every now and again, her heart quickened with the insistent memory of his arms about her, his kiss and the way he had rested his cheek on her hair with a kind of contentment. And all the time she heard the echo of his voice declaring that he would keep out of her life. She heard the words over and over again with painful clarity.

She did not want him out of her life, she knew. He had brought a new excitement and a new awareness into it. She felt really alive, tingling, glowing with anticipation of she knew not what!

Daisy sighed, suddenly weary. She sank into a chair and leaned back her head and closed her eyes. Gavin's face was etched very clearly on her eyelids.

He had kissed her and she had known that he wanted her with that fierce flame that had leaped in her, too. It was frightening, but she could not help feeling that it was right, meant to be. It seemed to Daisy that she had belonged in that embrace since the beginning of time.

Hadn't she always known the feeling of his arms holding her, the sensation of his warm mouth on her own, the sound of his deep voice saying the kind of things that every woman wanted to hear? Hadn't she always known the heavy beat of his heart against her breast and the throbbing passion that set up a swift echo in her own body? In her dreams, perhaps . . . but hadn't it always been Gavin Fletcher who filled those dreams long before she knew that he really existed?

That face, strong and sensual with its slight hint of arrogance and the warmth of the mouth with its slightly mocking tilt and the dark eyes that always seemed to hold just a lurk of gentle laughter. The hands with the strength and the sensitivity so skilfully blended. Daisy shivered suddenly, thinking of those hands on her body, caressing and persuasive, the hands of a lover. She thought of his body, so strong and muscular for all its lean build, so ardent and urgent and demanding that a woman could not help melting before the power and the passion.

He had held her and kissed her—and it had been far better than any dream. But Daisy was just a little afraid of this new and exciting reality.

She ached for him and she knew it was not love. Loving began in a small way with liking and trust and friendship between two people. Loving grew slowly and surely from a foundation of warm affection and understanding. Loving lasted.

There was a different name for the emotion that Gavin Fletcher stirred in her, she knew. One day, she hoped to combine the two. Loving *and* longing. But it would not be Gavin. For one thing, she did not really like or trust him and she did not think that they could ever be friends . . .

The doorbell shrilled. Daisy's heart missed a beat. It

was too early for Joanne who might have forgotten her key for the umpteenth time. Could it be Gavin—and was it likely that he would come to see her after saying that he would keep out of her life?

She flew to the door-phone on wings of hope. 'Yes . . . ?' She was breathless.

'Daisy? It's Richard.'

'Richard. Oh . . .' She was ashamed of the sudden flatness of her tone. 'I'll come down.'

She felt tired and grubby. She was wearing her oldest skirt and a rather skimpy blouse, good enough for cleaning the flat, but not very suitable for receiving visitors. Not that Richard would mind—or even notice, she thought wryly.

She supposed she was fond of Richard. He seemed to have been around in her life for some time without meaning very much. A girl had to have someone to take her to parties or the occasional meal at a restaurant or to dance with her at a disco. Not that Richard was much good at parties for he was a very serious young man, and he could not afford to take her out to eat very often and his dancing left much to be desired. But somehow he seemed to be the only man who stayed in her life despite the fact that she gave him very little encouragement.

Richard did not need encouragement. He took it for granted that they were friends and that he was always welcome at the flat and that she was always available to go out with him. He took it for granted that she would marry him one day, too, when he could afford a wife.

Daisy knew it, but it seemed so distant that she did not bother to put him right. When the time came, she would explain that she did not love him and could not marry him and Richard would shrug his broad shoulders in philosophical resignation and look about him for someone equally suitable to be a doctor's wife, she thought without resentment.

Richard was tall and stocky with the build of a useful rugger-player. His reddish-gold hair fell in a heavy thatch across an intelligent brow and frequently needed cutting. He had warm brown eyes and a nose that had been broken in a rugger scrum at school and which gave an attractive irregularity to his pleasant features. He had a rather shy smile which was the first thing that Daisy had noticed and liked about him before she discovered that it was deceptive.

For he was not at all shy or lacking in self assurance. It never occurred to him that anyone might not like him or want his company or would not listen when he talked. It was rather an appealing quality, surprisingly. It did not seem like arrogance. He was like a friendly puppy who never doubts his acceptance into the family circle or his place on a favourite chair.

He kissed her lightly. Then he followed her up the narrow staircase, remarking as he often did on the danger of the worn linoleum and the state of the peeling wallpaper.

'Tea . . . or beer? I think there are some cans of lager in the fridge,' Daisy said, wishing she felt better pleased to see him.

He took off his jacket and threw it down on the sofa in his usual untidy fashion. As he went into the kitchen for the lager, Daisy picked it up and took it into the bedroom to put on a hanger in the wardrobe, thinking that he and Joanne would make a fine pair.

'How did you know I was home?' she called, dreading the answer.

Richard came to the door of the bedroom, a can of beer in his hand. 'Sent home, weren't you? It's all over the hospital.'

'Oh, *damn*!'

He shrugged. 'What did you expect?' He took a draught of the cold lager. 'How did you manage to upset Sally Sweet that badly?'

'Without even trying,' she said bitterly.

Richard looked at her steadily. 'There's a lot of talk about you and Fletcher,' he said with apparent unconcern.

Daisy sat down on the side of the bed, fiddling with a button of her blouse. 'I can imagine.'

For a moment, he said nothing. Then he said: 'Not much fun for me, Daisy. Everyone knows that you and me . . . well, we're friends. I mean—you're *my* girl, aren't you? I wouldn't like to repeat some of the things that have been said to me this afternoon.'

'Look, Richard, I'm sorry,' she said with sudden impatience. 'But I can't help what people are saying! It's nothing to do with me.'

'You *have* been going out with Fletcher, I suppose?' He smiled his shy smile.

Daisy realised that he was embarrassed about asking but needed to know. She sighed. 'No.'

'It's just talk?'

'Well, of course it is! What makes you think that someone like Gavin Fletcher is likely to bother with me?' Her tone was tart.

He looked across the room at her with a rueful light in his brown eyes. 'I'd like to think that someone like you wouldn't bother with Fletcher,' he said quietly.

It was a reproach and Daisy cursed the unconscious

betrayal of her impulsive words. She knew that he was hurt—and so was she that he obviously did not believe her. It did not really matter, of course. But he should know that she did not tell lies.

'This is so silly,' she said wearily. 'A man does something as meaningless as wearing a couple of daisies in his button-hole and everyone thinks he does it to tell the world that he fancies me!'

'Does he fancy you?'

Daisy could not help the slow, warm tide of colour that stole into her face. 'How would I know?' she prevaricated.

'But you do know.'

Chipping away with that obstinate persistence, wearing her down, slow but sure. The methods he brought to his work and his medical studies. He would be a conscientious doctor, never accepting the obvious, always looking for a possible alternative to a snap diagnosis. Admirable . . . but irritating when he applied those methods to his private life.

'All right! So he fancies me! What does that mean? Everyone knows what he is!' she said, a little defensively, wondering why she felt that she had to defend herself when she had done nothing wrong and Richard did not even have the right to question what she did. They were only friends, after all, nothing more, now or ever!

'It wouldn't mean anything at all if you hadn't been out with him last night,' he said, rather slowly. He drained the last of the lager and placed the empty can in the middle of the dressing-table. 'Andrew saw you together. Coming out of the Kingfisher.'

Daisy knew Andrew. The two men were friends and shared a small terraced house with three other students, two of them girls, a practical and platonic arrangement that suited them all equally well.

She knew Andrew and how reluctantly honest he must have sounded and how sincere he would have been in feeling that Richard ought to know the truth. And it *was* the truth. She had been with Gavin Fletcher outside the Kingfisher, walking along the High Street, crossing the road to turn into the small and well-lit side street. It was inevitable that they should have been seen. She felt like saying *so what*? with a defiance that insisted on her freedom to do as she pleased. But that would hurt Richard even more and Daisy did not want to hurt anyone.

'I don't expect to be seen with him again,' she said quietly. So much fuss about nothing, she thought impatiently. It did not even merit an explanation.

'Well, I think that's wise, you know,' he approved in evident relief. '*I* know you aren't that kind of girl, but . . .'

'No.' Daisy cut him short. She rose and moved towards the door, wondering why she sensed a kind of tension in him.

Richard checked her with a hand on her shoulder. 'I wish you were at times,' he said, a slight smile about his lips. She glanced up at him, startled by the unexpected words. He bent his head to kiss her. For the first time, there was a hint of more than friendly affection in the pressure of his mouth.

Daisy backed away. 'Well, I'm not,' she said firmly. She had the oddest conviction that he was not convinced. Did he really think that she had kept him and every other man at bay only to fall a ready victim to Gavin Fletcher's persuasive charm? And did he feel that it might reward him to be rather more ambitious in his pursuit of her?

'I don't want to lose you,' he said abruptly. 'I love you . . .' He put his arms about her and drew her towards him, kissed her again.

Daisy was fond of him and much too gentle, much too kind-hearted, to push him away and tell him that he must not love her because she could never love him.

She allowed him to kiss her, poised to break free if he began to make demands. He had never said anything to her about loving in the past. Daisy did not think that he loved her . . . not really. He had merely felt threatened by the talk about her and Gavin Fletcher at the hospital and so he had allowed his emotions to sweep him into saying more than he truly felt.

Men were so perverse, she thought wryly. He had seemed to have very little sexual interest in her all these months and she had been comfortable and content in their relationship, liking him well enough and relaxed in his company because he did not demand anything more than her friendship and affection. Now, just because another man who was notorious for his many affairs had suddenly shown a degree of interest in her, Richard had decided to find her sexually attractive.

His kiss became more searching and she was abruptly aware of the rising sexuality in his embrace. She decided it was time to break away.

'Richard . . .' she warned, gentle but firm.

He stifled the protest with his lips. His hand slid inside her blouse, seeking the soft breast. Daisy tried to pull away, but he was strong, holding her firm. She put her hands to his chest.

'Love me,' he said urgently, against her lips. 'Let me

love you . . . I want you very much.' He was breathing hard, control slipping.

Daisy was too inexperienced to know that she was in danger. She was annoyed, but not at all afraid. She was ice-cold, unmoved by his kiss or the touch of his hand on her breast, and so she felt she was in command of the situation.

It might have been a very different matter if it had been Gavin's arms about her and Gavin's lips setting her senses in a whirl and Gavin's body urging her own to response, she thought, and was surprised to discover how cool and clear her mind was at this moment.

Richard moved swiftly, urging her towards the bed. The edge of it caught her behind the knees and she fell with him on top of her. Winded, she began to laugh. To her, it really was funny that Richard of all men, serious and steady and rather ponderous, should be throwing himself upon her in passion.

'Damn you! Don't laugh at me!' he said in a sudden fury of rage and longing, his body heavy and hard and urgent. 'Do you think I can't be as good as Fletcher when it comes to this kind of thing, damn you . . .'

His mouth was hot and hungry as he kissed her, forcing open lips that did not want to respond. Daisy began to feel just a little frightened. For this was not the Richard she knew. This was not the Richard who had seldom kissed her with warmth and certainly never touched her body in sexual overture. This was a stranger who had thrust the blouse from her breasts and was now tugging at her skirt in a near-frenzy of desire.

She tried to throw him off, heart racing and the blood singing in her ears. She refused to believe that he would force her if she did not yield. She refused to believe that she was in any real danger from him. This was Richard, she reminded herself . . . Richard, her friend!

She did not even know what had triggered so much passion. She had not been encouraging or at all provocative. She was astonished.

His body moved against her in a series of jerks . . . and was still. A little sound that was half-sigh, half-groan escaped him. Then he turned his head abruptly, ashamed and angry that he could not contain that fierce passion.

He did not resist when Daisy thrust him away on a sudden surge of anger. Free of his weight, she moved fast, scrambling to her feet and putting the distance of the room between them, fastening her blouse with shaking fingers and thrusting it into the waistband of her skirt. She was flushed, bright-eyed, trembling. She was appalled and very angry and she did not think that she would ever forgive him.

'I think you'd better pull yourself together and go,' she said stonily.

Richard slammed the bed with a clenched fist. 'I love you, Daisy,' he said, his voice muffled as he lay face down on the bedspread.

Her lip curled. If that was loving then she rather thought she preferred the straightforward wanting of a man like Gavin Fletcher. At least it was honest and it did not force itself where it was not wanted!

She went from the room and into the kitchen. Still trembling, still furious and deeply shocked by a new and not very pleasant experience, she stood at the window, arms folded tightly across her breasts, struggling with a little shame.

For there must be an unconscious sexuality about her

that could attract a rake like Gavin and turn a nice person like Richard into a raging beast so unexpectedly. Perhaps it had taken Gavin's kiss to awaken that sexuality. Perhaps its lingering effect had roused Richard without her knowing. In any case, she would take care not to be alone with him or any other man again. In fact, she did not think that she wanted any man to make any kind of love to her, tender or violent, ever again!

Richard knocked tentatively on the kitchen door. She did not open it and she did not answer when he called her name, low and hesitant. A moment later, she heard the front door of the flat open and close . . . and realised that she had been holding her breath. She let it go on a sudden rush.

She leaned forward to look out of the window and watched him walk along the pavement. She did not really relax until he was completely out of sight.

The end of a beautiful friendship, she thought heavily. Something more to lay at Gavin Fletcher's door! Suddenly, Daisy put her hand over her eyes to press back the tears. But the sobs were welling from deep down in her being.

She cried without really knowing why. Nothing had happened to her, after all . . . except that she had grown up just a little more. She felt a mingled pity and contempt for Richard who had been a victim of his own passions. And she felt a certain contempt for herself for she suspected that her reaction to the whole episode would have been entirely different if it had been Gavin Fletcher who had wanted to make love to her . . .

She was just taking a casserole from the oven when Joanne arrived home. Daisy smiled at her friend, taking care not to seem anything other than her usual self. She

had applied cold water to her eyes and did not think that
they betrayed her tears. And she had changed into a cool
dress of lemon silk and impulsively, not really knowing
why, thrust the old skirt and blouse into a brown paper
bag and rammed them into the kitchen pedal-bin.

'Smells good,' Joanne approved. 'Chicken?' She put
an arm about Daisy, hugged her. 'I don't deserve it after
letting you down over the food last night.'

Daisy suspected that the affectionate hug had nothing
to do with the events of the previous day. She looked at
her friend with a wry smile. 'You've heard.'

'That you had a barney with Sister Sweet and she sent
you off the ward? Yes.' It was not in Joanne's nature to
beat about the bush.

'Bad news travels fast.'

Joanne smiled, shrugged. 'And gets highly exaggerated on the way to its destination. It isn't the end of the
world, Daisy. Your past record is on your side, you
know.'

'I hope you're right.' Daisy began to lay the table.

Joanne went to change out of her uniform before they
sat down to eat. Daisy wondered if her friend meant to
mention the rumour about herself and Gavin Fletcher
that must have reached her ears as well as everyone
else's by this time. The grapevine was probably the most
efficient part of the famous Hartlake Hospital!

Joanne came into the kitchen. 'You've been busy.
Everything gleams.'

'It needed it.'

'And you needed to work off a bit of steam.' Joanne
smiled her understanding. She levered the lid of the
pedal-bin with her foot and dropped an empty lager can
inside. 'Had a visitor?' Daisy blushed to the roots of

her hair. 'I'm not prying,' Joanne said hastily, rather startled.

'It wasn't Gavin Fletcher!' Daisy said, very tart, knowing that Joanne had discovered the empty beer can in the bedroom. She would not blame anyone for leaping to conclusions, she thought, rather bitterly . . . even Joanne who was her friend and knew her so well. Thinking of her swift and startling response to Gavin's embrace, she wondered if she knew herself as well as she should . . .

'Do I detect a faint note of regret?' Then as Daisy turned swiftly with a militant sparkle in her blue eyes: 'Sorry! Only teasing!'

'So you have heard that as well?'

'Can you doubt it?' Joanne was blunt.

Daisy sighed. 'I know. It's all over the hospital.'

Joanne hesitated. She was fond of Daisy and knew just how trusting, how inexperienced and how very vulnerable she was . . . and she was a little anxious. Wisely, she decided to say nothing. Warning her about a man like Gavin Fletcher might only make her all the more determined to melt into his arms.

They had eaten and cleared away the dishes when Joanne suddenly remembered that she had a note for Daisy. She leaped up and rummaged in her handbag for several moments before she came across the white envelope.

She gave it to Daisy. 'Here you are! A porter passed it on to me, but he didn't seem to know where it came from. I expect it travelled a roundabout route to find me. Anyway, it's clearly for you and quite a few people know that we share a flat.'

Daisy looked at the envelope, rather curious. Her

name was written across it in bold, confident handwritng. She did not recognise the hand. She picked up a knife and slit the envelope and drew out a single sheet of paper, folded in half.

There was no heading and no signature.

'. . . *I've used my influence with Sister Sweet,*' he had written. '*You may return to normal duty on Fleming tomorrow morning and Matron won't hear anything about the matter from her. I wish I could say the same for the grapevine which seems to be very busy. Please believe that I really regret the whole business. You have my promise that I shall stamp on the rumours just as effectively as you stamped on my poor daisies.*'

'What's that?' Joanne asked, leaning forward to look at something that had fallen out of the letter.

Daisy looked down at her lap. Folded between the sheet of notepaper had been a single, long-stemmed daisy, carefully picked and still looking remarkably fresh. She was suddenly choked with a very foolish emotion.

He had sent her a daisy . . . and she was reacting as though it was a bouquet of beautiful, long-stemmed red roses . . . the flowers of love!

CHAPTER SIX

DAISY duly presented herself at the door of Sister's office, very punctually. Her apron was spotless, newly donned when she arrived on the ward. A nurse's apron was recognised as the symbol of being on duty and Sister Sweet was very fussy about clean aprons. Nothing could be more correct than her neat little cap, set at just the right angle atop her shining braids.

She knocked and waited, feeling like a naughty schoolgirl. But she knew that she would rather face a chilly Sister Sweet than report to Matron for a scold that would be registered very carefully in her files.

Bidden to enter, she went into the office. She stood before the wide desk, trying to look as penitent as possible, while Sister Sweet continued to write busily across a sheet of paper. Daisy studied her senior with a new interest, wondering just what kind of influence Gavin Fletcher had used in her favour. She could not imagine Sarah Sweet unbending very much even in the face of his disarming and very charming smile.

But she could visualise her as being quite attractive out of uniform, with that gleaming roll of rich, dark hair allowed to fall about her face, its heavy mass softening the rather hard features. And she had a lovely smile, even if it was seldom in evidence on the ward. Lovely eyes, too, but they looked up at Daisy with very little warmth in them and she hastily dropped her lashes, realising that she had been staring.

'Well, Nurse Palmer,' Sister Sweet capped her pen. 'I see that you received my message.'

'Yes, Sister. Thank you, Sister.' Hands demurely clasped behind her back, Daisy crossed her fingers against inadvertently saying or doing something to undo all the good that Gavin Fletcher had obviously achieved on her behalf.

Sarah Sweet studied her thoughtfully. She was a very pretty girl with a sweet personality and she promised to be an excellent nurse if she was allowed to finish her training. She had been a little surprised to learn that the girl and Gavin had known each other so long and so well.

Their respective families were friends, it seemed, and Gavin had promised to keep an eye on the girl when she came to Hartlake. No harm in that, of course—as long as it was just a friendly eye and he had assured her that his intentions towards Nurse Palmer were strictly honourable. Certainly she had not heard of anything going on between them until now, and the grapevine was very quick to remark such things. Either he had been unusually circumspect or he was telling the truth.

It must be a new experience for Gavin to take a merely platonic interest in a young and pretty nurse, she thought dryly. She had known him for years, without ever being fool enough to fall for his charm. Not that he had tried to coax her into bed at any time. Not pretty enough, Sarah admitted, without resentment.

They had been friends, and were still friends in an occasional kind of way. The occasional friendly word in passing, the occasional dinner or visit to a theatre, the occasional meeting at the house of mutual friends. Very easy, very undemanding—and nothing at all to interest the grapevine.

She supposed it was natural that the girl had confided in Gavin. Perhaps she had been a little hard on her. She *was* a worker and she was very good with the patients and certainly she had not found any fault in her until yesterday. Something on her mind, she had said—and Gavin had pleaded her case on much the same lines. A romantic upset, he had implied. Girls of that age were so susceptible and so sensitive. He was sure that Daisy would take care not to let her personal problems affect her work in future. If Sarah would relent, allow the girl to return to the ward as though nothing had happened . . . she had not yet sent in a report to Matron, had she?

Sarah hadn't—and she had allowed him to persuade her, a little amused to think of Gavin feeling so responsible and so concerned for the welfare and the career of a junior nurse. He usually had only one thought in mind where a pretty junior was concerned!

He really was an incorrigible rogue, but very attractive and very much nicer at heart than most people would allow him to be. Sarah knew it—and because she wished the nicer side of him was more in evidence to weigh against the undeniable rakishness of his general attitude to her sex, she was pleased that he had taken up the cudgels on Daisy Palmer's behalf. She hoped the girl appreciated it.

Studying the rather anxious face and noting the slight smudges beneath the blue eyes that hinted at a bad night, Sarah decided that she probably did. There was a great deal of good in the girl, no doubt. She was certainly much too good for the Gavin Fletchers of this world. But he apparently looked upon her as no more than a family friend and so she was probably safe from the kind of attentions that usually threatened the junior nurses where he was concerned· . . .

'I decided to let you return to the ward because Dr Fletcher assured me that you were really very sorry to have let me down so badly,' she said coolly.

'Yes, Sister.' Daisy decided that it would be wise to say as little as possible and let her senior do most of the talking.

Sarah looked at her, not unkindly. 'It was a bad day for you, I gather. Well, these things happen to us all and sometimes it isn't easy to put them out of our minds when we come on duty. But the patients and their needs must always come first, you know. That is the first essential of nursing and if you cannot grasp that and adhere to it then I'm afraid you are in the wrong job.'

'Yes, Sister. I'm sorry, Sister.' Daisy thought she would dearly love to know just what reason Gavin had offered up for her 'bad day'—and knew she dared not ask. But there was a quite unmistakable note of sympathy in Sister Sweet's voice.

'You do *like* nursing, I take it?'

'Oh yes, Sister.' It was fervent and sincere.

Sarah nodded. 'You'll make a good nurse one day,' she said, meaning it. 'You have a great deal of heart as well as common-sense and I've watched you with the patients. They like you and you obviously like them and that's important. I hope you won't make the mistake of allowing that heart to make a fool of itself over some worthless man. We lose too many good nurses that way. However . . . you'd better go and start rounds with Nurse Parkin.' She glanced at the watch she wore on her apron bib.

'Yes, Sister. Thank you, Sister.' Daisy turned to the

door, thankful it was over. She did not doubt that it would be forgotten. Sister Sweet was not the type to bear a grudge.

'Oh, Nurse . . .'

Daisy turned back. 'Yes, Sister?'

'You have been very discreet about your friendship with Dr Fletcher. I had no idea that you knew each other so well and I must say that it pleases me that you've never given any sign of it on my ward. You obviously do appreciate that personal feelings are out of place in a busy hospital, so we'll say no more about yesterday's lapse. I won't mention your relationship to anyone, of course. It's very much your own business—and I feel sure that I can rely on you to go on being discreet.' She smiled warmly.

Daisy was more taken aback by that glowing and totally unexpected smile than by the discovery of the "relationship" she enjoyed with Gavin Fletcher. It was only as she closed the door of the office and made her way to the ward that she wondered what on earth he had been saying to the woman.

But with the euphoria that came with the relief of emerging from the shadow of disgrace, she suddenly did not care. He had obviously convinced Sister Sweet that she did not deserve to be punished and that was all that mattered!

'Welcome back to the fold!' Patti gently nudged her in the back with the trolley that she was trundling. 'I don't know how you got away with it, but somebody pulled some strings.' She grinned at her friend. 'No names, but a certain doctor was closeted in the office with our Sally for some time yesterday afternoon.'

'I don't know what you can possibly mean,' Daisy

said, very demure, but eyes and heart were dancing. For he must have had a reason for ensuring that she stayed on Fleming—and couldn't it be that it allowed him to see her regularly? As Sir Leonard's registrar, he was a frequent visitor to the ward.

They started on the rounds of bedmaking, pulse and temps, fluid charts and blood pressures, tidying the ward in readiness for doctors' rounds and Daisy tried very hard to keep her mind on what she was doing and not to watch the clock and the ward doors as the time for Sir Leonard's round drew near.

She wrapped the arm bandage tightly about a patient's arm and reached for the stethoscope to take his blood pressure. 'Missed you yesterday, Nurse,' Mr Dennis said, rather sly. He was a friendly young man who had been admitted with a duodenal ulcer and was on bed rest and a gastric diet.

Daisy did not mean to be drawn. 'Even nurses have time off occasionally,' she returned lightly, squeezing the bulb and carefully watching the level of the sphygmomanometer.

'Thought you weren't coming back to this ward,' he suggested.

'Now why should you think that, Mr Dennis?' Daisy spoke rather absently, intent on listening for the systolic murmur. Then, satisfied, she released the pressure and returned the stethoscope to its box on the locker. 'I love you all too much to leave you,' she said lightly, reaching for his chart from the bottom of the bed to enter the reading.

'That isn't what I heard,' he said with a grin. 'Isn't a certain doctor more of an attraction than we are?' Daisy looked up swiftly, a little colour creeping into her face. 'I reckon I'm in the wrong job,' he went on cheerfully. He was a lorry driver. 'Put on a white coat and a professional manner and a chap gets all the girls running after him, seems to me.'

Daisy smiled. 'It only takes six years and a lot of hard work to qualify, Mr Dennis,' she said sweetly. 'And we are always short of doctors. I ought to warn you that ulcers are an occupational hazard for them, too, though.'

'Is that a fact? Oh well, then I guess they deserve a few perks,' he retorted, unabashed.

Daisy moved to the next patient, hoping that she was not going to spend the better part of her day running the gauntlet of that kind of comment.

There had apparently been a great deal of speculation about her sudden departure from the ward and nurses were apt to exchange little items of gossip during the ritual of bedmaking or while they were serving meals. Patients had nothing to do but take notice and listen to what was going on around them and gossip had a way of travelling very quickly from one ward to another, from department to department, via the confusing labrynth of corridors and flights of stairs and the constantly ascending and descending lifts.

There was an awful lot of to-ing and fro-ing by doctors and nurses and ancillary staff in a busy hospital like Hartlake and that partly explained the efficiency of its grapevine. It was also due to the enthusiastic if mysterious interest that everyone took in the merest hint of romance or liaison between a doctor and any member of the nursing profession. It was frowned upon and therefore it thrived . . . and half the fun seemed to lie in speculating whether or not the affair would fizzle out before it reached Matron's ears. It was always the nurse who was scolded and warned and sometimes sacked. Hartlake adhered to old traditions and an old-fashioned code of conduct for its nurses.

Daisy suspected that at least one of the nurses on Fleming had enjoyed her discomfiture and must certainly have noticed and remarked those daisies in the registrar's button-hole. Pamela Mason was a second-year from her own set who had recently set her cap at Gavin Fletcher and failed, for he liked to make the running. She was probably jealous of his rumoured interest in a nurse on the same ward. Somehow it was all over Hartlake that she was the man's latest flirt, Daisy thought wryly.

Whether by accident or design, Sister sent her down to X-ray with a patient who had a pulmonary infection just about the time that doctor's rounds were due to begin. Daisy did not know whether to be glad or sorry. She found herself wanting very much to see Gavin Fletcher again. At the same time, she was a little disconcerted by the feelings that he seemed to have stirred in her. From all that she had heard of him, it would be a mistake to like him too much and perhaps she ought to discourage him if he continued to show interest. But, remembering his last words to her, he might not take the least notice of her in future, she thought, heavy-hearted.

The patient was expected and the radiographer was waiting for him. 'Mr Marsh from Fleming? All right— leave him with me! How do you feel this morning, Mr Marsh? Breathing not too painful? We won't keep you long.' She straightened, smiled at Daisy. 'We'll send him back with a porter when we're finished . . . I know you're rushed off your feet on Fleming.'

'We are rather busy,' Daisy agreed, about to turn away.

'Just a minute.' The girl looked again at the second-year stripes on the cap and the ash-blonde plaits beneath it. 'Aren't you Daisy Palmer?'

Daisy stiffened. 'Yes.'

'I thought so.' She smiled, friendly but rather amused. 'Getting yourself talked about, aren't you? Aiming too high, you know—that's the trouble!'

Daisy was annoyed and didn't see why she should conceal it. 'It's a pity that the gossips haven't anything better to do than spread a pack of lies about the place!' she said tartly.

'Oh, I know, it's awful the way they can shred a reputation in no time at all,' the girl said, sympathising. 'Don't let it worry you too much. It might be you today but it will be someone else next week where Gavin Fletcher is concerned!' She added, rather mischievously: 'Give him my love, won't you?'

Daisy hurried from X-ray, fuming. She knew it was stupid to be cross, to flare up when people teased. It was a sure way to encourage everyone to believe that there was some truth in the rumours. But it was hard to be calm and to ignore the banter that did not always mean to be malicious.

Herself this week—and someone else next week. No doubt that was true and she ought to find some comfort in the radiographer's careless assurance. But she did not want to think that his interest in her was so fleeting, so casual, so entirely sexual—although she knew perfectly well that it would be the height of folly to suppose anything else!

Turning into one of the wide main corridors of the

hospital, she ran into a nurse from her set who was working on Paterson, Women's Surgical. They were friends and she could not rush past without a word.

Phyllida kept her for a few minutes with eager and overtly curious questions about her work on Fleming and her rapport with Sister Sweet and the other nurses on the ward. Then she said with seeming carelessness: 'Of course, you see a great deal of Gavin Fletcher on your ward, don't you? What's he like? Really, I mean? One hears such exaggerated stories about him, but I guess he can't be all bad if you're going out with him.'

'Look, Phyllida, I'm *not* going out with him and I wish you'd squash the rumour that says I am whenever you get the chance! It's just a silly story that someone started and there isn't an ounce of truth in it!' She was rather cross and very firm.

Phyllida was taken aback by the touch of anger. But she thought she understood. Any girl in love was bound to be sensitive and it couldn't be very easy for Daisy to have fallen for a rake like the handsome Dr Fletcher who seemed to have so many girls dangling on a string. She had always avoided the kind of romantic entanglement that might threaten her nursing career. Daisy was a dreamer but she was not a fool. But Phyllida supposed it must be exciting to have attracted the attention of a man who could take his pick from so many of the nurses at Hartlake. Falling in love with a doctor was an occupational hazard for any nurse, after all.

She smiled her sympathy. 'All right, love. I'll do what I can,' she said, knowing that any such attempt would be greeted with derision. Everyone knew that she was Daisy's friend and would naturally try to defend her from the gossips. 'But you can't keep secrets in this place, you know. I don't think it's worth trying! No one could be more careful than Ruth Challis but everyone knew about her affair with Oliver Manning. I suppose you do know that they're engaged . . . ?'

Phyllida offered the titbit of news rather hopefully although it had broken some days before and was already being overshadowed by the titillating talk of a romance between Daisy and the incorrigible Dr Fletcher. It was just possible that her friend had been too taken up with her own affairs to have heard, she felt.

Ruth Challis was ward sister on Paterson. Oliver Manning was a consultant surgeon, handsome and clever and much admired—and with a considerable reputation for chasing the women without getting caught in the marriage trap. Rather like Gavin Fletcher, in fact. The announcement of his engagement to the rather reserved sister had shaken Hartlake to its foundations.

Daisy was not very interested, although she knew and liked Sister Challis. Her own disturbing feeling for a man too much like Oliver Manning for comfort and the realisation that she was unlikely to bring *him* to his knees in loving was more on her mind than the engagement of sister and surgeon.

'I must go,' she announced, preparing to move on. 'We're rather busy on the ward and I'm not in Sister's good books just now as it is!'

'I heard about that,' Phyllida returned with disconcerting promptness. 'She sent you off after she caught you in the linen cupboard with Gavin Fletcher, didn't she? You *were* running risks, Daisy!' There was almost admiration for her friend's daring in her tone. 'I hope he's worth it!'

Daisy was speechless.

She whisked off in such a fury that her starched apron crackled all the way along the corridor—and it did not improve her temper when two medical students turned as she passed them and began to whistle softly to the tune of '*Daisy, Daisy, give me your answer, do . . .*' She wondered bitterly if her name was written in bright red letters across her forehead!

How on earth did people know that she had been in the linen cupboard with Gavin Fletcher? It was quite untrue that they had been discovered by Sister and she was sure that no one had seen them go in or come out! It *could* have happened, very easily. They had been lucky. So how was it generally known? Only through Gavin himself, she thought bitterly, thoroughly dismayed.

He must have recounted the incident with great relish to his friends. Daisy wondered that she had been so near to liking him, trusting him, when she only had to remind herself of his reputation to know just how little respect he had for any woman.

Flirtation was never anything more than an amusing game to his kind and it seemed that he did not care how badly he damaged a girl's good name!

Crossing Main Hall, Daisy caught the eye of Jimmy, the Head Porter. He knew everyone and everything. The big man winked at her knowingly and looked as if he could say a great deal on the subject of young nurses who foolishly succumbed to the lures of doctors who had anything but marriage on their minds. After thirty years at Hartlake, he had probably seen it all too many times, she thought heavily.

Women could be such fools. Well, she did not mean to fall for a charmer who thought he had only to smile and any girl he wanted would fall into his arms. She would have nothing more to do with Gavin Fletcher.

It was not one of Sir Leonard's days for his Hartlake patients and so Gavin had done the round that morning with the houseman and Staff Nurse Trish King. The round over, the houseman was busy with the history of a new admission and the staff nurse was hunting in Sister's office for a patient's fluid chart that had unaccountably been missing from the case notes.

Gavin waited on the ward, hands thrust into the pockets of his white coat, stethoscope dangling. For once he was unconscious of the interest that he aroused in the nurses who passed him as they went about their work. Daisy was not among them and he wondered what had happened to her and if she had received the note that he had sent by a very roundabout route to avoid comment.

Sister Sweet had been busy in a side ward with a very ill patient when he arrived on Fleming. She had sent the staff nurse to accompany him on the round. Gavin had not cared to ask Trish King if Daisy had reported for duty that morning as advised. He did not want to add any fuel to the fire of speculation that seemed to be burning much too brightly already. He had his ear very close to the ground and he knew that there was a lot of talk about his supposed interest in the girl and he was sorry for it. Any girl who encouraged him must expect the gossips to have a field day. But Daisy could not be said to have encouraged him, he thought wryly.

He knew how swiftly the grapevine seized on the least hint of romantic interest in a casual exchange between any doctor and a nurse, on or off the wards. But it was surprising that it was making so much of something that had never happened. Did they never tire of his affairs, he wondered wryly? Or was it only that Daisy was obviously not the kind of girl who usually got herself talked about? He was much inclined to curse the impulse that had led him to pick those daisies.

The swing doors opened and Daisy came into the ward, stopping short as she saw the tall man with his dark good looks and lean, lithe build. She did not like the way her heart turned over, defying her resolution to forget all about him.

Gavin quickened at sight of the slight girl with her flower-like prettiness. She was well-named, he thought, oddly moved. He was tempted to retract on the assurance to stay out of her life, remembering the way he had felt when he held her, kissed her. Suddenly he wondered if she was the girl he had been looking for all his life . . .

There was a militant sparkle in the vivid blue eyes and her chin flew up in a way that told him she was about to attack. For such a shy and gentle girl, she had a great deal of spirit. He raised an eyebrow and his own eyes held a warning. For Sister had come out of the side ward and was looking in their direction.

He did not smile, but he looked as though he meant to speak. Daisy did not give him the chance. 'You're despicable!' she threw at him, low and very fierce. 'Keep out of my way or you'll find yourself in trouble, Dr Fletcher! Don't think I won't report you to Matron if you ever speak to me or touch me again! Because I will—and I'll enjoy doing it!'

'God, you're a firebrand!' he said, amused, eyes dancing. 'You've all the makings of a Sister Booth, you know. And you'll end up a dried-up old maid like her if you don't give a man the chance to get to know you, girl!'

Sister was descending on them with a very purposeful air. Daisy abruptly decided that there was nothing to be gained by a slanging match with a thoroughly hateful man who did not seem to understand that she despised him.

Hastily, she turned to answer the conveniently-timed call of a patient . . . and Gavin turned to Sarah Sweet with a disarming smile and a light word that allayed the suspicion that the couple had been on the verge of quarrelling on her ward!

CHAPTER SEVEN

DAISY was late leaving the ward. She had stayed to help
with an admission from Accident and Emergency. The
patient was an orthopaedic case, a teenager who had
fallen on a building site and damaged his back. It had
taken some time to settle him comfortably once he had
been put into traction. He was in a great deal of pain and
it had touched Daisy's tender heart to watch him fighting
the unmanly tears. No more than seventeen, the boy had
begun his first job after leaving school only a few days
before and had lost his footing on the scaffolding.

She had carefully washed the grime and dust from the
young body and brushed the thick mop of hair, dark and
curling and reminding her of Gavin. He was a good-
looking lad despite the cuts and bruises that marred his
eager young face. He was lucky that he had only fallen
some twenty feet. X-rays showed several slight fractures
of the vertebrae. It might have been very much worse. He
was a keen footballer and his particular anxiety seemed
to be that he should be fit to play by the time the football
season began.

Daisy came out of the hospital by Main Hall, pausing
to exchange a few words with Jimmy, who never seemed
to go off duty. As she descended the wide stone steps to
the pavement, she drew her cloak about her shoulders
against the rain. She was seldom aware of time or
weather when she was on duty, like most nurses. There

were so many more important considerations in a busy hospital.

Joanne was out. She had left a note to say that she did not expect to be back until late. Daisy took off her cap and flopped into a chair and kicked off her shoes, deciding that it *would* be fish and chips tonight—when she had sufficient energy and inclination to walk back to the High Street to get it!

She padded into the kitchen to put on the kettle. Returning to the sitting-room, she saw a letter propped on the sideboard. It was for her and it had come by second post. A letter from home. Daisy suddenly felt a wave of homesickness. It was over two months since she had seen her family. With an older brother lecturing at Lancaster University and a younger brother in the Army, Daisy had quite understood when her parents decided to sell the house on the outskirts of London and move to a part of Devon that they had always loved. But it did mean that she could not see them as often as she would like.

She made tea and carried the tray into the sitting-room. Her head was aching slightly and she was glad to unbraid her hair and shake it loose. Then, curling up on the lumpy sofa with her long legs beneath her, she opened her letter and settled down to enjoy it.

She had not read more than the first few lines when there was a knock at the door of the flat. She rose and went to answer, expecting it to be one of her neighbours on the borrow. Visitors to the house had to announce their identity over the door-phone and were then admitted. It was an excellent security device for a houseful of women and worked very well, except on the odd occasion when someone was on the way out of the house just as a visitor was mounting the steps to the front door. Then, very often, she would allow him or her to enter on the strength of a friendly word. Which must have happened in this instance, Daisy thought, as she opened the door to Gavin Fletcher.

She was pleased to see him in that split second of time before she remembered—and Gavin saw that flicker in the vivid blue eyes and smiled. He thrust flowers into her arms, having paused at the flower stall that always stood on the pavement by the main entrance to the hospital.

He was not usually a man of impulse, but he had found himself doing all manner of impulsive things just lately . . . such as wearing wild flowers in his lapel and hanging about Main Hall in the hope of catching her on the way from the ward and buying up half the contents of a flower stall in the hope of pleasing her. But she did not look very pleased, he thought wryly. 'Peace offering,' he said.

Daisy was taken aback. It was the last thing that she had expected from him—and it meant that she could not close the door on him as she rather wanted to do.

'You'd better come in,' she said, ungraciously. Feeling slightly out of her depth and rather wary of him, she would have liked to leave the flat door wide open. But that would constitute an open invitation to her neighbours to wander in at will and she did not want any of them to know that Gavin Fletcher had found his way to her flat, quite uninvited.

She felt absurdly small against him, standing in her stockinged feet, half-buried by flowers. She wished she had not let down her hair, too. She felt vulnerable and knew she looked like a schoolgirl with the long hair rippling in waves over her shoulders.

'I'll find some vases,' she said vaguely and disappeared into the kitchen. She put the flowers on the draining-board and looked about her helplessly, wondering if they had any vases. Nurses saw plenty of flowers on the wards and seldom bothered with them at home.

'I didn't expect to find you on your own, you know,' Gavin said, appearing in the doorway. Tall, broad-shouldered, impressive, he seemed to fill the tiny kitchen. Or was it just that she was much too aware of him, Daisy wondered, a little flustered.

'Joanne is out.'

He raised an eyebrow. 'Again? I'm beginning to wonder if she exists,' he said, teasing.

'Of course she does!' Triumphant, Daisy emerged from the depths of a cupboard with a massive cut-glass vase that would take all the flowers with room to spare. She filled it with water and thrust the stems into the vase with scant respect for flower arrangement. She was a believer in the theory that they would settle themselves quite happily if left to do so! 'They're lovely . . .' She turned, vase in hand, to find him regarding her steadily. Her heart missed a beat. She suddenly found herself fighting an odd little fear, a stirring apprehension. 'I'm sorry you've chosen the wrong evening to call,' she hurried on, a little breathless. 'But I'm going out myself very soon!' It was true, she argued with her bristling conscience. She *was* going out—for fish and chips!

Gavin knew her nervousness, her floundering. He was touched by that little shyness, that obvious inexperience, even while he was rather dismayed by her blatant distrust of him.

He nodded. 'Fair enough. I expect you want to get ready for your date, and I'm in the way.' He moved towards the door. There had been more than enough women in his life and there would be plenty more if he could not have this one, he knew. But he wanted her rather badly—and more than was wise in view of her youth and inexperience and his own reputation!

'Thank you for the flowers.' Daisy knew it was sensible and very much safer to send him away without even the least hint of encouragement. She wished she did not feel so mean, so ungracious, so unkind to distrust him so openly. 'But I wish you hadn't brought them!'

'No strings attached,' he said lightly. 'I'm just making amends. I seem to upset you without even trying and half the time I don't know what I've done. I feel I ought to apologise now for anything I might inadvertently do tomorrow. I daresay you'll feel that you've some reason to fly at me like a fish-wife.' He smiled at her gently.

Colour flooded into her small face. 'You make me sound very unreasonable.' Just then she could not think of any good reason to keep rebuffing this very attractive man whose smile could stir her heart so strongly.

He shrugged. 'All women are unreasonable, Daisy. It's a fact of life.'

He knew too much about women, she thought, resenting it, abruptly remembering why she was so determined to keep him at a safe distance. He flaunted his knowledge, too, quite unashamed of the life he led, the women he seduced. It hurt her quite unaccountably to think of those women, meaningless perhaps, but knowing more of him than she ever would.

He used her name too freely, too, making it sound like an endearment on his lips. Oh, he had charm, but that was part of the stock-in-trade of any rake, after all. He was very persuasive in the way he smiled, the way he made a woman feel that she was the only one in the world. And perhaps she could be the only woman in his world for a little while, Daisy thought rather wistfully. She could not help being flattered by his seeming interest and his persistence. He must like her, she thought, very reluctant to suppose that he only wanted her because she would not admit to wanting him.

Gavin noted the fleeting changes of expression across that pretty, candid face. She was very sweet, really enchanting.

'Why were you so cross?' he asked gently. 'I've been puzzling about it all afternoon.'

'You talked too much,' she said, a little curt.

He raised an eyebrow. 'Did I? What about—and to whom?'

'Snatching a kiss when no one's looking is all in the day's work to you, isn't it? It means nothing more than that. I shall never understand that men find it so easy to brag about such things to their friends.' Her tone was sharp, contemptuous.

His brows came together in a swift frown. 'You've got it wrong again, Daisy. I don't kiss and tell, not in any circumstances,' he said firmly.

She looked at him doubtfully. She would like very much to believe him. 'All right,' she said, rather grudgingly. 'But someone knew . . .'

He shook his head, smiling. 'I'm not going to apologise for something I didn't do, Daisy. What a girl you are for thinking the worst! Is it just me or don't you trust any man?'

'I don't trust *you*, anyway.' The retort came promptly even as she wondered, deep down, if she really meant it. Despite everything, she could not help liking him, feel-

ing drawn to him. There was more to this man that she
had believed at first. He might not be anything like the
man of her dreams, but somehow that seemed a very
misty figure compared with the real and forceful and
rather compelling Gavin Fletcher.

'Silly girl . . .' He touched her cheek in a light, very
careless caress and then turned towards the door.

Daisy's heart had somersaulted in very odd fashion as
she met the indulgent, almost tender smile in the dark
eyes. The touch of his hand had melted the very bones in
her body. She wished she did not recall so vividly the way
he had kissed her. She wished she did not want him to
kiss her again, to rouse her to that swift response that
had been so new, so exciting. She wished he was not
quite so attractive.

He was going and Daisy did not want him to go. It was
perverse and foolish, but she wished there was a way to
keep him without swallowing her pride too obviously.
He was leaving as casually as he had come, accepting his
dismissal without protest or resentment. Heaven knew
why he had come at all, brought her that mass of flowers,
if he wanted nothing in return! He was a strange,
unpredictable man.

'I should offer you a drink, I suppose,' she said
abruptly. 'I'm not in that much of a rush to get ready to
go out.' She indicated the bottles on the sideboard.
'There's whisky or vodka or vermouth, some lager, I
think. I don't know what you like.'

'Is it an important date?'

'Sorry . . . ?'

'This man you're meeting tonight. Will it matter if you
don't go? I'd like to take you out for a meal, wherever
you want. You'll never trust me if you don't get to know

'me as something more than Dr Fletcher, will you?' His smile was very warm. 'You could try calling me by my first name, for instance.'

Suddenly things were happening too fast. The merest hint of encouragement and he was rushing her into going out with him for the evening. Heaven knew where *that* would lead, she thought, her pulses quickening. But she had to admit that the prospect of going to a decent restaurant for a meal with a very attractive man appealed much more than solitary fish and chips in the flat.

'I'm not sure . . .' She was doubtful, tempted.

Gavin moved towards her slowly. Daisy looked up at him, a little shy, a little unsure. He reached out his hand to cradle her head, very gentle, and suddenly the air was electric. The chemistry between them sparked into instant, leaping sexuality. Very experienced, very sure that she was reacting to him as forcibly as he was reacting to her, he knew that he must not say or do anything to shatter the moment. One wrong word, one wrong move . . . and she would always be wary of him.

'I'm not sure, *Gavin*,' he corrected lightly, a smile in his dark eyes. 'Take the first step, girl. It isn't so hard.'

'Gavin . . .' she echoed obediently, tingling at the continued touch of his hand, the warmth in his voice, the promise in his eyes. She knew that she had taken the first step towards more than friendship, but the approval in his smile made it all worthwhile, she discovered, relaxing.

He sensed the sudden yielding. Desire stirred in him suddenly, very strongly. Careful not to alarm her, not to lose the ground he had gained, he wound his fingers in the thick, silky mass of her hair and bent to kiss her, resisting the urge to catch her close in passion.

Daisy found it difficult to breathe for the hammering of her heart, the rising excitement that made her body clamour for the urgency of his embrace. He kissed her, the merest, teasing hint of a kiss, so light as to be almost meaningless. She was flooded with disappointment.

She drew away from him. 'I shall have to change.'

'Then you will come?'

'Yes.'

He was suddenly exultant. 'Good girl! I was beginning to wonder if you knew that word!'

She laughed at the triumph in his dark eyes. Her heart was ridiculously light and she found that she was looking forward to spending the evening with him. 'I don't use it very often,' she warned.

His dancing smile caught at her heart.

'Words aren't always necessary,' he said softly and with a great deal of meaning. He moved towards the decanters. 'May I help myself?'

'Of course! Relax with a drink while I get ready . . . I won't be too long.'

Daisy was just a little conscious of his male presence about the flat as she hastily stripped out of her uniform frock and filmy underwear, donned a thick towelling robe and went through to the bathroom.

He had switched on the television set and settled himself on the sofa with his drink. He did not even glance up and Daisy was reassured. At the same time, she thought ruefully that he was obviously well used to lounging about a girl's flat while she showered and dressed. He was entirely at ease and very much at home.

On the way back from a quick shower, damp and

sweet-scented, she paused to study him. He seemed to be absorbed in a documentary about the troubles in Ireland. But he *was* aware of her, she realised. He held out his hand, smiling, not looking at her. Momentarily Daisy hesitated. Then she went to him and put her hand into his, a little shyly, her heart beginning to thud.

It pleased him that she was beginning to trust him. He was very tempted to draw her down to him. But he realised that this shy and very virginal girl could not be rushed into bed for all the urgency of his wanting. He carried her hand to his lips, kissed it lightly—and let her go against all his inclinations. He knew by the way she released her pent-up breath that she had been apprehensive.

He rose abruptly. 'It's raining quite heavily. I'll walk down and bring the car to the house while you dress. Come down when you're ready.'

Daisy was relieved by his casual manner. She was also aware of a vague disappointment and scolded herself for offering such a man even a hint of dangerous encouragement. She would have had only herself to blame if it had led to something that must not happen!

He was waiting in the car as she came out of the house, hesitated on the steps. He sounded the horn fractionally. It was a sleek, expensive silver car and Daisy remembered that she had once heard that he had a private income besides the salary he earned as a Senior Registrar. To many girls, that was an added attraction. It made Daisy feel just a little more shy of a man whose background was probably very different to her own.

He leaned across to open the car door.

Daisy slid into the passenger seat beside him. She noticed that his dark hair was damp, tightening into the curls that made her fingers itch to twine around them. 'Did you get very wet? It's a foul night.'

'It doesn't matter about me.' He brushed aside her concern. 'But it would have been a pity if that very pretty dress or its very pretty wearer had been caught in the rain.' The car slid smoothly away from the kerb, headed for the High Street and the bright lights.

Daisy wondered why she had not expected him to be a thoughtful, considerate, attentive man who knew just how to give a girl a wonderful evening. He could not be so successful with women if he did not have a great many attractive qualities, after all. She was beginning to understand how it was that girls were foolish enough to fall in love with him. Her own heart was threatening to capitulate before his charm, she thought wryly. It had probably been a mistake to go out with him, but how could she regret the enchanting intimacy of the little Italian restaurant with its exquisite food and sparkling wine or the warm admiration and flattering attention of a very attractive man?

They danced on the small square of polished floor to the soft, dreamy music of a trio and he took care that she was not jostled by the other dancers on that limited space. He held her very close, but his embrace was undemanding. Gavin was in very strict control of the situation. Daisy relaxed, liking him, enjoying the slow movement of the dance and the warmth of his body moving against her own.

Perhaps she had drunk a little too much of that lovely wine, she thought, slightly euphoric and just a little reckless. But he was very nice. She liked the way his dark hair curled on the nape of his neck. Dancing with him, she could allow her fingers to slide into those tantalising

little curls. She liked his strong good looks and the dark
eyes with their little lurk of laughter. She wondered if he
was laughing at her. Well, she did not mind. It was very
tender amusement. She liked the mobile mouth and felt
very tempted to lay her own mouth against it in provaca-
tive invitation, remembering his kiss and its effect on her
senses. And she liked his hands, so strong and sensitive
and nice to hold, exciting in the way they held her body,
keeping her close to him.

She nestled even closer, laid her head on his shoulder . . . and stumbled over his feet. She chuckled.
'Sorry . . .'

'Time to take you home, girl,' Gavin said, amused.

'Not yet,' she protested.

'Daisy, it's nearly one o'clock and the staff want to go
home.'

With a little shock of surprise, she suddenly saw that
the place was almost empty and only she and Gavin were
still dancing. Time had seemed to stand still while she
moved in his arms.

'Oh . . .!'

He laughed, drew her from the dance floor to collect
her bag from their table. 'Come on—or you'll be sleep-
walking on the ward tomorrow!'

'Heavens, yes! I'm working.'

'So am I, my sweet,' he said dryly. He settled the bill
with a handful of notes and exchanged a few friendly
words with Luigi, a former patient who always welcomed Dr Fletcher and his variety of pretty companions
to his restaurant.

'Where do *you* live?' Daisy wanted to know, a little
sleepily, turning her head to look at Gavin as he drove
through the still-busy streets of London, wet pavements

gleaming beneath the lights and a surprising number of pedestrians hurrying in the rain.

'I've just moved into a house in Parmenter Street . . . one of those little terraced cottages that were built at the beginning of the century but have been very well modernised. I bought it from Lester Thorn. Know him? Used to be Wilmot's registrar but he's doing research at the Central these days.'

'The one who was keen on that staff nurse on Paterson,' she said sleepily. 'Jessica Brook. She was running around with Clive Mortimer until that scandal about him and a first-year.'

'I'm glad that the grapevine isn't only busy with *my* affairs,' he said, dryly amused.

Daisy lapsed into silence, discovering how much she disliked that legion of meaningless affairs which attached to his name. Her spirits sank as she thought that she might too easily be just one more of them. She wished she did not like him so much . . .

Gavin brought the car to a halt. 'Safely delivered to your door,' he said lightly. He touched her cheek with his long fingers. 'Still awake?'

'Yes . . . just about.' She mustered a small smile, wondering why she felt so depressed so suddenly.

'I'd help you to bed, sweetheart,' he told her with a twinkle in his dark eyes. 'But I rather think that friend Joanne would cramp my style. Assuming that she exists . . .'

'When you meet her you'll forget that *I* exist just as they all do,' she said impulsively and with just a hint of a bitterness she had not realised she felt.

Gavin slid an arm about her shoulders, drew her towards him. 'I don't think you're so easily forgotten, you know,' he said, meaning it. He found her enchanting, quite delightful . . . and very tempting.

He touched his lips to the soft hair, the smooth temple, the curving eyelids and the shapely little nose. He found her lips and kissed her, long and lingering, seeking warm response. He felt the slight body tense and then relax against him with a little sigh . . . and he relaxed, too, suddenly confident.

Daisy knew that she had been waiting for his kiss, aching for it. It was all that any woman could want, sweet and stirring and sensual and yet not so demanding that it alarmed her or so insistent that she was compelled to draw away.

She wanted that kiss to go on for ever. It opened up a new and quite magical world. For his lips were very warm and tender and giving.

She felt his hand at her breast and her body stirred. His hand closed over the soft mound beneath the thin frock and his thumb moved in slow caress across the nipple. Red-hot excitement shafted through her loins, exciting but frightening. She checked him, pushed his hand away. 'No.'

'I want you, girl,' he said against her lips, low, compelling, vibrant with desire.

'Please, Gavin . . .' She drew back, reluctant but firm.

He looked into her eyes and there was very meaningful warmth in his expression. 'Please, Daisy,' he said softly, intently. 'Come home with me tonight. I want you very much . . .'

'No.'

He sighed. He put his hand in the long, silky hair and touched her lips, fleetingly, with his own. He felt her quiver. 'Darling, you want me,' he said, a little impatient. 'I know it! Don't run away from life, Daisy. It catches up with you in the end. You can't want to stay a virgin for ever!'

She jerked her hair from his hand and he knew that too much wanting had led him into error. She opened the car door, gathered up coat and bag.

'Goodnight, Gavin.' She looked at him with a little anger in her eyes. 'It was a lovely evening—until you had to spoil it!'

'You've got a lot to learn, girl,' he said wryly.

'I don't have to learn it from you!' Hurt by the attitude that she ought to have expected from him, she walked away from the car without a backward glance.

CHAPTER EIGHT

DAISY knew she must fight the growing need that was so much more than sexual. She liked Gavin Fletcher too much, she thought ruefully. She thought about him day and night.

Going about the day's work on the ward, she found that she was thinking about him and longing for the strength of his arms about her and the smile in the dark eyes that told her that he liked and wanted her. If only his kind of wanting was similar to her own she might feel that she could encourage him, she thought unhappily.

But he was a sensual man who liked women too well and enjoyed them whenever the opportunity offered. As a handsome and very eligible bachelor he was entirely free to do so, of course. Daisy had no right at all to resent the women in his life. And it was very silly to want to be one of them, she told herself firmly.

For the moment, Gavin wanted her, and Daisy was just a little flattered and warmed by his interest, although she suspected that it was only her stubborn virginity that drew him like a magnet. She doubted if she could hold him very long if she yielded.

He seemed to tire of women very quickly and there was always another pretty girl to take the place of the last, if the grapevine was to be believed. She wondered why she liked him so much when the Casanova type had never recommended itself to her. Was he really so much nicer, so much more attractive, than any other man she had known?

Richard, for instance . . .

She had not seen Richard, and she doubted if he would try to get in touch with her until the memory of that afternoon had faded. He had embarrassed and shocked her—and she had offended him. Having been fond of him in a rather sisterly way, and sometimes very glad of his company and escort, Daisy was sorry for that sudden and unsuspected glimpse of a very different Richard to the one she had always known.

It was strange to realise that his unexpected passion had offended her so much, and yet the same kind of wanting in Gavin's embrace had stirred and excited her to instant response. She supposed it was all due to chemistry. Gavin attracted her in a very physical way. Poor Richard had repelled her because she had just never thought of him as a potential lover.

She wondered if it was a kind of perversity in a woman that made her respond instinctively to a rake like Gavin Fletcher while ignoring all the many excellent qualities of someone as well-meaning and respectable as Richard.

Richard was definitely husband material, she knew. Gavin enjoyed himself too much with a constant variety of girls to sacrifice his freedom and his independence for the sake of settling down with one for the rest of his life.

For someone like Daisy, loving was synonymous with marriage. Therefore she had no intention of falling in love with a man like Gavin. The danger to her impulsive heart was much too real—and so it was best to go on discouraging him.

She kept out of his way as much as she could, disappearing into sluice or kitchen or side ward at first sight of him, backing in the opposite direction if she saw him coming along a corridor towards her, finding all sorts of reasons for escaping from the ward when she knew he was due to visit it.

Sister Sweet thought she was being discreet and trying to discourage the gossip that had got it all wrong about their friendship. She did what she could to ensure that they had very little contact on the ward. Daisy supposed she ought to be grateful. Instead, she could not help wondering if her senior was just a teeny bit jealous. It was very likely that Sarah Sweet did have a soft spot for him like too many women, after all.

She had discovered through listening to a couple of the juniors talking in the sluice that the ward sister and Gavin Fletcher were old friends and that he had dated her occasionally. She could not always be so stiff and unbending and ice-cold, Daisy thought, but perhaps it was just that Gavin had the power to melt any woman into warmth.

Apparently, one year he had been her escort to Founder's Ball, the highlight of the Hartlake year when the hospital ran on a skeleton staff so that as many as possible could attend the gala occasion. It was a magical evening when etiquette was relaxed for once and no one frowned if a senior doctor danced with a first-year nurse or a ward sister flirted with a medical student, and even Matron had been known to whirl about the dance floor to a quickstep in the arms of a consultant, proving that she was human as well as surprisingly attractive out of uniform.

Founder's Ball was looked forward to for weeks and talked about for months afterwards. It had been responsible for the beginning or ending of many a romance between members of the staff. Perhaps it was appropriate that it should be such an important date in the calendar for the place that too often lived up to its nickname of Heartache Hospital!

There were changes on the ward. Old Mr Benbow had been transferred to the geriatric unit in the hospital annexe and he had gone reluctantly, protesting that he wanted to return to his council flat. Last-minute apprehension and the natural dislike of the old for relinquishing responsibility for their lives to efficient strangers had overcome his earlier fear of a return to poverty and loneliness.

Mr Paine was due for discharge, but did not want to leave, insisting that he still needed the occasional use of the oxygen mask. It had become a pyschological need and he would have to be encouraged to do without it. But that problem need not concern the hospital. He had made a good recovery and no longer needed nursing care, and his bed was already earmarked for another patient.

The big man in the side ward had been taken back to the Cardiac Unit after the emergency team had been called to him in the night. He had only just survived that second heart attack and he was very ill.

The gall-bladder suspect had been transferred to Currie, Men's Surgical, for removal of the offending organ. And poor old Mr Lane had died, slipping away quietly in his sleep, escaping at last from the scourge of the disease that had imprisoned his frail little body for so long. He had been a favourite on the ward, but with the admission of new patients there was very little time to miss one patient among the many who came and went in a busy hospital like Hartlake.

Gavin made an unexpected flying visit to the ward one afternoon to see a patient, accompanied by the house-man. Daisy was busy with the young boy with the injured back as he came down the ward with his purposeful stride. He paused at the next bed.

Daisy wondered if he would smile or speak. He did not. She hoped it was preoccupation or discretion and not dismissal. Her heart had turned over with uncom-fortable rapidity at sight of him, but she went on with her work as though he did not exist, like a well-trained nurse aware of Sister's eye upon her.

He spent some time with the patient, talking to him, examining him, discussing treatment with the house-man.

Daisy concentrated on the boy in the bed, settling him as comfortably as she could for the weights of the traction. Gavin did not even glance in her direction.

But when she had tidied the locker and left, swishing down the ward and through the swing doors like a nurse with nothing on her mind but her work, he rose unhur-riedly. With a word of reassurance for the sick man with the stubborn chest complaint that he hoped to cure, he strolled from the ward with the houseman.

Daisy came out of Sister's office after checking the work-book and saw him standing by one of the long corridor windows, looking down at the hospital garden that was bright with sunshine and busy with people and beginning to be festooned with bunting by some of the medical students in readiness for Founder's Week.

He turned, looked at her with a slightly raised eye-brow, and she knew that he had been waiting to waylay her. There was just the hint of a smile in his dark eyes.

Daisy refused to smile at him. It would be a sign of

weakness, of forgiveness—and she was not ready to forgive him for being so attractive and so nearly dear that all her defences threatened to crumble at a touch.

But she paused, looked at him enquiringly. 'Is there anything I can do for you, Dr Fletcher?'

She was very cool, very distant, reminding him of the great gulf between a senior doctor and a junior nurse and her reluctance to bridge it as he wished.

His smile deepened. 'Wrong time, wrong place,' he said lightly. 'How about tonight—my place?' His drawl was teasing, but very warm, hinting at persuasion.

He saw the rounded, stubborn chin tilt and watched the slow tide of colour creeping into her small face. She was so pretty, so touchingly determined to keep him at bay. Suddenly he wanted to cradle that face in both hands, to kiss her very gently. He thought of most women with sensuality rather than tenderness. But this girl seemed to have a certain quality that caught at his heart. He liked her very much—or he would not keep trying, he thought rather wryly. There were plenty of pretty girls at Hartlake and most of them were more encouraging than this one, but he continued to want this one!

'You never give up, do you?' Daisy was tart because she was so near to weakening. There was a little trembling inside her at that look in his eyes, that particular warmth in his voice. But she knew that it was a dangerous response for a girl like herself who needed to mean much, much more to a man than just a casual conquest, just another triumph for his sexual attractions.

'Are you saying *no* again, girl?' Gavin sighed in mock despair. 'I thought I'd coaxed you into the occasional yes!'

He turned everything into a joke, she thought wearily, and almost wished that she did not take life and loving quite so seriously. After all, she might be missing out on the fun and the excitement and the careless adventure that seemed to be so important to her friends. But she could not flirt, could not treat loving so lightly as Joanne and Patti and almost every other girl at Hart-lake.

She turned to leave him before Sister or Staff Nurse came along and caught them talking. His hand shot out to grip her slight shoulder and she looked at him swiftly, startled, a little indignant.

'Daisy, I'll give up right now if that's really the way you want it,' he said, suddenly very serious. 'Just say the word! Wanting you is getting to be painful and I'd as soon end it now if I'm never going to have you!'

Daisy was shocked by the intensity of desire and frustration in the words. She supposed that some girls might be overwhelmed by the force of his wanting. She was only bleakly aware that it was blatantly sexual desire without the least hint of affection or even real liking. She did not expect a man like Gavin Fletcher to speak of loving, of course, and she was thankful that he did not resort to that strategy to get what he wanted as some men did. But a girl liked to believe that she mattered for more than her body, she thought with sudden anger, born of pride.

'I shall go on saying no, if that's what you mean,' she said steadily, knowing that she could never give herself to any man without some measure of loving between them. She was not hanging on to her virginity out of sheer bloody-mindedness as he seemed to suppose. She had simply never met a man she could love and she meant to wait for that day to dawn, she told herself very firmly.

His hand dropped to his side as Patti came out of the ward with her arms full of dirty linen. Gavin strode off down the corridor without another word and Daisy was left to wonder if she had been too adamant. But it was humiliating to be regarded as little more than a sexual object by a man she liked too much for peace of mind, she thought wryly, knowing that he was becoming a definite threat to her happiness at Hartlake.

'There's no such thing as privacy on a hospital ward,' Patti said lightly. 'Not even in a linen cupboard. I might have walked in on you, after all.'

Daisy looked a little conscious. 'How is it that everyone seems to know about that?' she demanded ruefully.

'Those daisies.' She smiled with affectionate understanding. 'The ones he was wearing on his coat that day. They must have fallen out and Pamela Mason found them in the cupboard, kicked into a corner, and your pen was on the floor, too.'

'My pen!' Daisy remembered losing it, but thought she had put it down on the ward. It had never occurred to her that it could have been dislodged by Gavin's sudden embrace.

'She'd make a good detective,' Patti said dryly. 'Anyway, as you aren't one of her favourite people and she fancies Gavin Fletcher herself, she put it round that you were in the habit of luring him into quiet corners and finally got caught by Sister who sent you off. Oh, I've got your pen, by the way!' She had been off duty for a couple of days and it was her first chance to return her friend's property.

Patti manoeuvred the bundle of linen under an arm

and drew out the distinctive pen that bore Daisy's initials from her apron pocket.

'Thank you.' Daisy was grateful to have it back for it had been a Christmas present from her parents and she valued it very much.

'Nothing to do, Nurses?' Sister Sweet's caustic tones reached from the swing door of the ward.

Patti bustled off with the dirty linen and Daisy was thankful that she had only been caught talking to her friend when it might so easily have been Gavin. 'I'm just going to put on a clean apron, Sister,' she said hastily.

'Well, be quick about it. I want you to collect a blood urea result from the Path Lab.'

'Yes, Sister.'

Making her way through the labyrinth of corridors in the basement to the Pathology Department, Daisy thought about Patti's explanation and recalled that she had not really believed Gavin's denial. She was contrite. He had said that he did not kiss and tell, she remembered. Perhaps she was too ready to distrust him. For it seemed that she had Pamela Mason to thank for the gossip that seemed to have reached every pair of ears in the hospital—except, hopefully, Matron's!

She might have been nicer to Gavin if she had known. She might have agreed to meet him that evening. For she had enjoyed the evening she spent in his company and he had certainly done all he could to make it very pleasant. She supposed she could not go on being angry with him for making a pass at her when almost every man in the world would have done exactly the same! Gavin was very much a man, after all . . .

Daisy's birthday fell later that week and it surprised her that so many of the patients knew about it. She suspected that Patti had been spreading the word. She was touched to receive an unexpected birthday card, signed by most of the patients, and one or two of the men pressed gifts on her, a box of sweets, a miniature bottle of brandy, a presentation box of stationery. She did not mind that they were passing on their own presents from visitors, knowing that they wished to express their thanks and sincere appreciation. Not of one nurse in particular, perhaps. But of every nurse who looked after their needs while they were in hospital.

There were cards and presents from her friends among the staff, too. She began to feel quite overwhelmed. Even Sister Sweet wished her a happy birthday with a surprisingly warm smile and allowed her to slip away from the ward rather earlier than she had hoped. Having the afternoon free, she meant to shop for something special to wear to Founder's Ball. She did not have a particular escort but was going with a group.

Daisy had left for the hospital before the postman called that morning and when she reached the house she found cards and letters from her parents and two brothers, more cards from other relatives and friends.

Joanne's present was sitting in the middle of the sofa when Daisy let herself into the flat—an enormous, dark-brown plush bear with gold-coloured ears and nose and paws. His appealing brown eyes gave him a very lifelike appearance and the card that dangled from a gold ribbon about his neck declared: *'If you're looking for a friend, I'd like to apply . . .'* It was so typical of Joanne. Daisy was touched by the warm generosity of the gift and delighted with its originality.

She read her letters and stood her cards about the room, warmed by the evidence of affection and friendship. She had found so many real friends since coming to Hartlake.

The door-phone buzzed. Daisy hesitated, tempted to ignore it, for she was not expecting anyone and she did not want to be delayed in going out. It buzzed again and she moved to answer. 'Yes . . . ?'

'Gavin.'

She was startled, not knowing whether to be pleased or dismayed. She had not seen him about the ward for a few days. 'I'm just going out,' she said uncertainly. She wanted to see him—and yet she didn't. She was all mixed up inside.

'You can spare five minutes.' There was a note in his voice that defied argument.

Daisy ran down the stairs, aware of that too-familiar excitement and apprehension. She opened the door, looked up at him, not very welcoming. 'What do you want?'

'Well, I don't want it on the doorstep,' he said, very dry.

She hesitated, stepped back. 'All right, come up. But only for five minutes,' she said firmly. She knew she was being ungracious. But that was better than letting him know the little leap of her heart at the sight of him.

Gavin stopped just inside the door, a smile quirking as he saw the gigantic bear. 'Who's your fat friend?' he quoted in his lazy, amused drawl.

She sent him a quick, appreciative smile. 'I'd introduce him if I knew his name,' she said lightly. 'But he hasn't been christened yet. I found him when I came in. He's a present from Joanne.'

He was encouraged by the sudden warmth in her smile, that hint of friendliness. He took a small box from his pocket, offered it to her. 'I'm on duty this evening. So I had to see you now. Happy birthday, love.'

The endearment was casual, but there was nothing casual about the expression in his dark eyes. He was finding it increasingly hard to ignore her growing importance.

Daisy was not looking at him or her heart might have leaped with very foolish hope. She stared at the little box on the palm of his hand, startled and oddly moved—and wondering how he had known that it was her birthday. She was very inclined to blame Patti once more!

With a fast-beating heart, she opened the box and drew out a slender gold chain. A gold heart swung from a tiny pivot, engraved with *Yes* on one side and *No* on the other. It was exquisite.

'Oh, Gavin . . .' she said, rather helplessly. She looked at him between tears and laughter.

'I thought it was appropriate,' he said lightly, smiling down at her. 'A man likes to know a woman's mood in advance. He doesn't make so many mistakes that way.' He took the chain from her fingers and put it about her neck, fastened it.

Daisy tingled all the way down her spine at the touch of those light fingers at the nape of her neck. He must have searched every jeweller's shop in the district to find just the right gift, she thought—and then had it engraved to suit the vagaries of their relationship. He was the most unexpected man, making it very difficult for her to go on keeping him at a distance, she thought wryly.

'It's lovely,' she said, a little unsteadily. 'But you shouldn't give me anything so expensive, Gavin. We hardly know each other!'

'You won't let me give you anything else, girl.' His eyes twinkled with sudden, teasing mischief. 'But I'm an incurable optimist. I hope that we shall know each other very well eventually.' He put a hand to the little gold heart, turned it to the *Yes* side.

Daisy wondered if it was perversity that kept him hanging about her or the challenge of her seeming indifference. Men like Gavin who usually got what they wanted from a woman with ease probably did not like to admit defeat. But it was baffling that he should want her when she had so little to offer—and there were so many girls who would not say no to him.

Resolutely, she flicked the heart so that the *No* side was uppermost once more. 'I shall disappoint you, Gavin,' she said firmly. 'I won't change my mind.'

Deep down, she knew it would be easy to be swept off her feet by his undeniably exciting interest. But. . . herself this week and someone else too soon! She was nothing special. How could she expect to hold him and she certainly could not hope to win his love! So how could she trust him? How could she allow herself to like him too much, to want him so urgently?

Gavin took both her hands, held them tightly. 'I wish you would,' he said softly. 'I can't stop thinking about you . . . wanting you!' It was an almost unwilling admission.

'Don't you say that to all the girls?' Daisy's tone was defensive for all its lightness. She did not believe him. She did not think that she really mattered to him. She was just a girl who had not fallen headlong into his arms like all the others and he was determined that she should. Daisy was just as determined that she would not.

But she wished that she did not want him so much. He was too much of a threat to her peace of mind. She did not like the way that her heart leaped at his smile, the way her body melted at his touch. It was too dangerous.

Perhaps if it had been only physical wanting, the kind of attraction that flared and died very quickly, she might have been tempted to risk everything for the sake of the excitement and the ecstasy she could find in his arms. But she was afraid of the feelings that he stirred. She was terribly afraid that she would lose her heart to this man—and she dreaded the inevitable heartbreak when he tired and turned away.

'I wish you'd trust me,' he said, a little angry. 'I've said it to a few girls—yes! There's no point in denying what everyone knows! But it's different this time.' His expression softened as he looked down at her. 'Stop fighting me, Daisy. I'm not so very bad, you know. Let me buy you a birthday drink tonight—and I won't even kiss you, I promise!'

She pulled free, resisting the throb in his voice, the appeal in the dark eyes that threatened to undermine her defences. 'No,' she said resolutely. But her heart was beating hard and her voice shook slightly.

Gavin looked at that proud face, the defiant tilt to the small head, and heard the determination in her voice for all its tremble. He felt as though he was hitting his head against a brick wall—and he was suddenly angry.

Damn her! He was near to loving for the first time in his life and perhaps he ought to be grateful for the obstinacy that kept him from such a danger. For loving was the first step on the slippery slope that led to marriage and he did not think that was for him, now or ever!

Damn her for that stubborn defiance, that prickly pride! Damn her most of all for the sweet charm and the shy innocence that had almost penetrated his armour and had certainly struck deeper at the heart of him than any girl he had ever known.

Annoyed, frustrated, not particularly caring in that moment if he ever saw her again, he turned to the door. 'Right! I won't ask you again, girl!'

Daisy wondered why she felt that she had hurt him. His pride, no doubt! No man took kindly to a rebuff and she had not even tried to soften it.

She felt just a little guilty. She did like him, after all—and couldn't she try to trust him . . . ? She said on a sudden impulse: 'Is it too late to say yes?'

He looked at her, quirked a slightly mischievous eyebrow. 'Meaning . . . ?'

Colour stole into her face. 'Meaning that I'd like to meet you for a drink,' she said firmly. 'Nothing more!'

Gavin flicked her soft cheek with his fingers in a gesture that might or might not have been a caress. 'I'll call for you just after ten. Okay?' Wisely, he did not try to take matters any further at that point, knowing that he would probably lose the little he had gained.

CHAPTER NINE

HE was early.

Daisy had been ready, watching the clock, for at least half an hour. But, woman-like, she flew to the mirror to check that face and hair and clothes were just right when she heard the sound of his car horn.

It had been difficult to know what to wear for a quiet drink in a pub. Naturally, she wanted to look nice, but she did not wish to be overdressed for a casual date. She had spent much of the evening selecting and discarding and finally settled on a simple frock of flowered silk. She had washed her hair and coaxed it into curls and she thought that for once she looked quite pretty. Of course, she was nothing beside the beautiful Joanne who always cast her into shadow, she reminded herself dryly.

Joanne had gone to a party. She had accepted Daisy's explanation that she was meeting a friend later in the evening without question. Joanne never probed.

Longing to fly down the stairs and into his arms, Daisy schooled herself to take her time, to seem cool and unconcerned and very casual. But she did wonder if her leaping heart would give her away as she came out of the house and saw the flicker of warm appreciation in his dark eyes. She felt a little glow of feminine satisfaction and smiled at him with rather more warmth than she had intended.

Gavin opened the car door. 'I was beginning to wonder if you'd changed your mind again. I'm never sure about you, girl.'

'You did say ten o'clock,' she reminded him.

He smiled. 'I pulled a few strings.'

'Where are we going?' Daisy asked as the car eased away from the kerb in the opposite direction to the High Street and the local pubs.

'My place. I've organised a meal and I remembered that you liked the wine we had at Mario's the other night. You don't object, I hope? It's been a long day and I feel that I've had enough of crowds.'

Daisy hesitated, apprehension stirring. But she had decided to try and trust him, she reminded herself—and it would be gauche and unsophisticated to admit that she was nervous of being alone with him.

'I don't mind,' she said quietly and not very convinced.

'Sure? We'll go to Mario's if you prefer it, as long as you give me time to change out of these clothes.'

Gavin was tired, rather tense. It had been a difficult day with more than the usual amount of problems. He would have liked to relax with a girl who did not insist on keeping him firmly at arms' length. A meal, a little wine and laughter, the release of the day's tensions in lazy, light-hearted lovemaking with someone who made no real demands on him was just what a man needed at the end of a hard day on the wards. He wondered at that perversity in him that kept him so interested in a girl who only promised to build up an even greater tension without any hope of release.

Daisy glanced at him, saw the pulse throbbing in his lean cheek, a sign of strain. He looked tired, too. She had caught the hint of impatience in his tone and did not blame him for it. It would not be surprising if he was already regretting that he was with her and not some other and more encouraging girl.

'I don't want to be too late tonight,' she said carefully. 'And you do seem to have gone to a lot of trouble . . .'

Gavin smiled. 'Relax, love,' he drawled, dark eyes dancing. 'I'm not setting you up for the big seduction scene.' He reached for her hand, pressed it. 'I do understand how you feel, you know. I'm not entirely insensitive. You feel that we have to be friends before we can be lovers, don't you?'

Daisy was grateful for the quiet words with all their reassurance. Her apprehension began to evaporate. She allowed her hand to lie in his clasp. 'I'd like to be friends,' she said, rather shy. 'But I don't know about anything more than that.'

He lifted her hand to his lips and kissed it lightly. 'We progress. From *no* to *don't know*. That's excellent.'

The terraced house was small but immaculate, cleverly modernised and very comfortable. It was a very masculine abode with its leather furniture and plain carpets and modern lighting, its expensive stereo and the very latest in video recorders. Daisy looked with interest at his books, his pictures, the exquisite pieces of Capodimonte statuary. She discovered that they had similar tastes in literature and music and art. He was easy to talk to, nice to be with. He was also a surprisingly good cook. Daisy enjoyed the meal but she was careful not to drink too much of the heady, sparkling wine. She thought he was a little amused by her caution.

Later, she studied him as he sorted through a pile of records. As soon as they reached the house, he had left her briefly to change into casual slacks and a thin sweater. He looked very handsome, younger and more approachable. Daisy warmed to him suddenly. His dark hair was rumpled and he yawned like a sleepy boy. She knew he must be very tired and wondered if she ought to suggest that he took her home. But was not so very late and it was pleasant to relax, to listen to the music, to feel so much at ease with a man who had not made any amorous advances such as she had expected and dreaded.

She wondered that she had been so mistrustful of him. After all, he was not a callow youth like Richard and she must not condemn him as a Casanova with nothing else on his mind but sex. Wasn't it possible that he would be content with friendship and liking and affection if that was all she felt she could offer? She had made her stand and it seemed that he was prepared to respect her for it. She felt sure that he liked her and that was heart-warming. For she liked him and felt almost tender towards him for proving that he could be in her company without sex rearing its ugly head.

Having chosen the records and set them to play, Gavin sat on the sofa and relaxed against the cushions, closing his eyes as the music filled the room.

Daisy felt piqued. She might not want him to make violent love to her, but she did not want to be ignored. She did not want to have to fight him off, of course. But she would not have minded too much if he had put an arm about her, kissed her. It was quite nice to be kissed by someone as proficient at it as Gavin, she thought wistfully.

He was so relaxed, so still, that she wondered if he had fallen asleep. The music was soft, soothing. Romantic music and muted lighting, a man and a woman together—stuff that dreams were made of, Daisy thought—and he was a million miles away. She wondered how he would react if she were to kiss him.

Woman-like, she toyed with the idea, half tempted and half afraid. Should she encourage him quite so much? Did she really want the evening to end so tamely without even a kiss as a souvenir?

She discovered that she was tense, tingling with a kind of excitement, stirred by a sudden ache of desire. It shocked her slightly to admit it, but she wanted him to kiss her, to hold her, to quicken her senses with his touch and his need. Her body recalled his kiss, the ardour of his embrace, and rebelliously refused to heed the warning of her level head.

She rose from her chair, heart thudding, scarcely knowing how a woman invited a man's lovemaking without seeming cheap. Gavin stirred and opened his eyes. Daisy wondered if she had really meant to make the first move. She pretended that she had been reaching for one of the record sleeves that he had left on the low table. He smiled at her with lazy, attractive warmth—and her heart tumbled.

On a sudden impulse, she knelt on the sofa by his side and laid a hand along his lean cheek, tenderly. She smiled into his slightly surprised eyes. Then she leaned forward to kiss him, shy but warm. There was no response. She hesitated. Then she kissed him again, pressing her lips to that sensual and so reluctant mouth with a little urgency. She was hurt and bewildered that he was holding out against her so unexpectedly.

'Hold me,' she said achingly.

He put his arms about her, but he held her so lightly that she found it hard to equate his seeming indifference with his eager sensuality of other times. Had he suddenly lost interest? She felt a shaft of anxiety. Had he found someone who did not say no to him with every other breath and therefore was content with just a platonic relationship where she was concerned?

Puzzled, she pressed her body against him, aching for his arms to tighten and hold her with warm reassurance. She was throwing herself at him, trembling and tremulous, and it seemed that he just did not want to know. Had she said or done something to offend him, to give him a disgust of her, to convince her that she was not the kind of girl he wanted in his life, after all? Poor Daisy racked her brain to think what it could be.

'I must take you home,' Gavin said abruptly. He was astonished by the sudden and very impulsive turn-about in her attitude to him. He was not disposed to take advantage of it. Girls who were carried away by their emotions and rather too much wine were apt to cry rape in the morning, he thought dryly.

She kissed him again, willing him to respond, trying to fire him with the flame that was burning so fiercely within her that nothing else seemed to matter. She thrust her fingers through the thick black curls, jerked almost savagely at his head. 'Oh!' she said, impatient, frustrated. 'I thought you wanted me, Gavin!'

'I hope you know what you're doing,' he returned quietly, wryly. 'Don't push me too far, girl. I'm only human . . .' He was taut, very tense.

For answer, she melted against him, all yielding softness that no man of flesh and blood could possibly resist. With something that was half-sigh, half-groan, Gavin caught her close with all the pent-up passion of a man who had tried to withstand but found it too difficult when she tempted him beyond endurance with her warm lips, her eager arms, her lovely and unexpectedly willing body.

His body was on fire, throbbing with the desire that she had fanned so deliberately. But she was such an innocent, so unaware of how close he was to losing all control, that he was afraid for her. She was too generous, too ready to give with that sensuous yielding, those eager, uncaring kisses. He knew that it sprang from an enchanting but dangerous innocence.

He kissed her, slow, very sensual, knowing just how to excite and delighting in the way her lips received him. She clung to him, eager, inviting.

'Come to bed, Daisy . . .' He was suddenly urgent. Her answer was the merest murmur of her lips against his neck, framing the word. But it was all he needed.

He rose, lifting her into his arms as though she was a mere nothing. Slight and slender, she seemed such a fragile, flower-like wisp of a girl that she caught abruptly at his heart.

As he moved towards the door, she said lightly: 'You don't have to carry me, Gavin. I won't run away.'

'I don't trust you,' he said, and she smiled.

He made easy work of the stairs and took her into the room with its big double bed. He laid her down on the coverlet and looked at her, unusually hesitant although he wanted her very much.

Daisy held out her arms, all invitation.

He had never hesitated to take what came his way in the past, with eager delight in the sexual encounter. He wondered what held him back now when he had wanted her since the first moment that he had become aware of this girl with her pretty face and enchanting innocence.

He undressed her with very gentle hands, as though he expected her to resist or protest. There was a kind of reverence in his touch. Her heart gave a leap as she heard him catch his breath in sheer delight when she was nude, then he bent to brush his lips across her tilting breasts as though he paid homage.

Daisy had expected to be afraid. She was not. She had expected to be shy, uncertain. She was not. It suddenly seemed right and natural that he should be the man to initiate her into the wonderful world of sexual delight.

She put both hands to his dark head, drew him to her and kissed him on the mouth. 'I want you,' she said softly.

Still he hesitated. 'Sure, Daisy?'

'Yes . . . oh, yes!'

He touched his lips to that soft and so sweet mouth. Then he drew away and pulled his sweater over his head, trembling with the need to control the surging passion before it overwhelmed him completely.

Daisy quivered with excitement. As he came down to her, her arms went about him in eager welcome. She drifted on a sea of enchantment as he kissed her, long and lingering, his body stretched beside her own. When he paused, seemed unsure, she took his hand to her breast in unashamed longing for his caress.

The touch of his hand aroused a delicious sensuality such as she had never known and did not want to end. She allowed the tide of wanting to engulf her as his lips traced the shape of her mouth, the slender line of her throat, the warm hollows of her neck and then moved delicately to the gentle swell of her breast.

'You're beautiful,' he said achingly. 'Lovely, lovely flower . . . darling Daisy.'

She smiled at the endearment, something to cherish. She put her hand to his head in a caress, stroking the thick, curling hair. Then her body arched in sudden, fierce craving as his lips hovered over the roseate bud of the nipple. She felt the sudden weight of his body and knew the urgency and the eagerness of his passion, matching her own.

She held him, filled with the aching need for fulfilment, knowing the longing to give as well as take. She trembled on the threshold between virginity and fulfilled womanhood . . . and suddenly, without reason, she was afraid.

It was too big a step to take. Supposing she failed him, disappointed him. He had known so many women and they must all have been more sensual, more experienced, much more clever than herself at loving without commitment. Daisy wanted with all her heart to give for his pleasure, his delight, his satisfaction—and her own. But she was abruptly afraid of the bond it must inevitably create between them.

She was on the verge of loving him. She *would* love him if she allowed him to sweep her into the magical, mysterious world of supreme ecstasy for man and woman.

Daisy was afraid to love him . . .

She buried her face against his broad shoulder, absorbing his warmth and masculinity. Her body tensed, resisting.

'I'm afraid,' she whispered.

Suddenly Gavin could not take her. It would be the easiest thing in the world, he knew. Every woman hesitated before the final surrender and he could overcome that hesitation and sweep her into a glorious yielding. But he could not do it.

He liked her too much and, odd contradiction though it seemed, he wanted her too much to take her in light and careless loving. She would regret it and he would never forgive himself, he thought wryly, fiercely quelling the urge of his body for satisfaction.

He kissed her, very tender. 'Then it isn't the right moment—and I'm not the right man,' he said quietly.

Daisy was shaken by his words, and as the urgency of desire began to lessen, she was deeply grateful. She did not think that many men would have understood, accepted, failed to be furious at that last-minute disappointment.

'I'm sorry,' She felt dreadful. She had been all provocation, all warm invitation, all eager surrender—and then she had refused him. There was an ugly name for women who did that kind of thing to a man, she knew, cringing inside, desperately hoping he would not think too badly of her, hate her. There had not been hate or anger in his quiet voice, she comforted herself. He had shown a rare and admirable understanding of her inner tension.

She had thought that he was dangerous and unscrupulous, not to be trusted, she reminded herself wryly. Now she knew that the real danger lay in her own sexuality, newly awakened and never suspected and rather frightening. Until now, she had never been deeply stirred by any man's touch. Until now, she had never understood the power and the glory that could make a woman forget everything in the arms of a man—the power of passion and the glory of giving to delight them both. Until now . . . and she had probably rejected the one man in the world who could transform a very ordinary experience into heaven here and now!

Gavin rose, dressed. The ache of wanting was persistent and painful. He doubted if she even realised the torment of sudden denial for a fiercely ardent man. She was too sweet and much too gentle to have inflicted it deliberately, he knew.

'Get dressed, Daisy. I'm taking you home.' He didn't realise that his brusqueness hurt her. He had only meant to reassure.

He went from the room. Utterly miserable, she hurried into the clothes that he had removed with such loving hands. He was waiting, car keys in hand, when she joined him. She did not know that he did not trust himself to say much and certainly not to touch her. She only felt that he was angry, thwarted, contemptuous of her behaviour.

When the car stopped outside the house in Clifton Street, she turned to him anxiously. 'I'm sorry, Gavin,' she said again, not knowing what else to say and thinking how inadequate words could be.

He smiled wryly. 'Some men might think that you're just playing hard to get. I know it isn't that. You're just following your instincts and they keep telling you not to get involved with someone like me.' He bent his head suddenly to kiss her, light and quick. Daisy thought it was entirely without meaning and shrank back. 'You're the kind who falls in love and thinks it has to be wedding bells,' he went on gently. 'I want you more than any girl I've ever known, Daisy. But that doesn't mean that I'll ever want to marry you. I don't think I'm the marrying kind, love. So I'm not the man for you—and you're clever enough to know it. Tonight nearly happened because you're impulsive, but virtue triumphed, after all.' He was wryly mocking. He ran his hands through his hair, sighed. 'I told you that I should stay out of your life, girl. In future, I will.'

Daisy was silent. The hurt started from somewhere deep in her being and spread in a fierce flame of agony throughout her body, worse than anything she had ever known. And it hurt most of all in the region of her heart.

She ought to be grateful for his honesty. He was being very frank, warning her that it would be madness to love him, telling her bluntly that he was incapable of regarding her as anything more than a girl he liked with a body that tempted him. Daisy felt as though a cruel hand was tearing the very heart out of her body—and wondered what she had expected of him? Hadn't she always known instinctively that it would be a mistake to allow herself to like him too much, to get involved with him? Hadn't she always known that he was the kind of man who could not settle for one woman in his life?

But a lesser man, knowing that she was a very green girl, might have strung her along with empty words and false promises until he had taken what he wanted and tired of it and then left her with heartache and humiliation. Gavin had too much integrity and strength of character and innate kindness. He was not a cheat.

Which only made it all the harder for her, Daisy thought bleakly. For he was a man that any woman would be glad to have in her life—if he loved her and could be loyal.

But Gavin admitted that he would never love her and he was certainly not the type of man to be loyal for long to any woman. He had said so with brutal frankness, refusing to allow her to cherish any false hopes or dreams about him or the future.

He cared enough to protect her from a very foolish heartache, it seemed. She knew that she would probably not see him again except as a stranger on the wards of Hartlake. It was the end of a dream. Their friendship had never really got off the ground and yet it had contrived to bring a real and lasting love into her life.

For poor Daisy was not standing on the threshold of loving any longer. She had toppled well and truly over the edge, she realised unhappily.

She loved him—and he had left her in no doubt that he did not want her love. He was backing away from the demanding intensity of an emotion that could never warm his own heart or make him feel that he wanted to spend the rest of his life in loving and caring and sharing.

Her heart welled with fresh pain.

Gavin saw the tears sparkling on her long lashes and the small hands, clenched so tightly that the knuckles gleamed. He felt a brute. But she was very young and he believed that she would soon forget him if he allowed her to do so.

He had been jaded by casual encounters with too many women who had meant very little to him. But Daisy was different. Daisy was a new enchantment that might too easily lead to loving—and Gavin did not feel that he was ready for that kind of commitment.

Besides, he knew himself very well and she deserved better than a careless rake like himself. She was sweet and lovely and much too good for him. It would be very wrong to go on seeing her, possibly encourage her to care for him, when he could give so little and she would probably give too much.

He touched his hand to her cheek. 'Goodnight, love,' he said lightly.

Daisy knew that he meant goodbye.

She did not know how she managed to smile at him and wish him goodnight with that same casualness of manner. She was thankful for pride in that moment. She could even turn at the top of the stone steps, key in hand, and wave a careless hand as the car moved away from the kerb.

But the tears were streaming down her face as she let herself into the flat, thankful that Joanne had still not returned from her party and she did not have to cope with the sympathy and concern and all the quivering questions that dear, thoughtful Joanne would never ask.

Numb with despair, she leaned against the door, and the sight of that absurdly big bear, perched on the sofa and patiently waiting to be noticed, abruptly reminded her that it was still her birthday. It wanted just a few minutes to midnight.

She put her hand to the thin gold chain about her neck, a memento of a man and a day that she would never forget as long as she lived.

Suddenly she sank to the sofa and buried her face and the hot tears in the warm, cuddly coat of the big brown bear.

CHAPTER TEN

'WE'LL have a party!' Joanne declared on a sudden inspiration.

Daisy did not glance up from her book.

Joanne looked at her friend, troubled. Daisy was in the doldrums and it was all due to the on-off affair with Gavin Fletcher. The grapevine did not seem able to make up its mind whether or not anything was going on between them—and certainly Joanne did not have a clue!

Daisy would not open her mouth on the subject of Sir Leonard's registrar and Joanne was much too tactful to ask questions. But she suspected that the note and that single, rather mysterious daisy, the flat-full of flowers and the delicate gold chain that Daisy wore about her neck had all been his doing, and she was rather intrigued.

It did not seem likely that a man who was famous for his many light-hearted affairs would persist in pursuing a girl who rebuffed him. Unless he really cared for her. Having heard a great deal about Gavin Fletcher, Joanne doubted that very much. Her innocent and much too intense friend was not the type to appeal to such a man except in passing. She had probably shown a great deal of good sense in refusing to have anything to do with him, Joanne thought, knowing that Daisy was just not sufficiently experienced in the ways of his kind.

But if she *liked* him, wanted him, indulged in her

romantic and rather touching dreams about him . . . ah, that was the rub, Joanne thought wryly. It was not always necessary to approve of a man to like him too much for comfort. The women who had fallen in love with rogues and optimistically assured themselves that reformed rakes made the best husbands were legion!

She decided not to notice Daisy's marked lack of enthusiasm. She brought paper and pencil to the table and began to make a list of likely guests.

'We didn't celebrate your birthday, so it's a good excuse for a party, as if we need an excuse!' she said brightly. 'Now . . . John, naturally.' She wrote the name of her latest admirer at the top of the list. 'Cathy and Paul. Richard, of course.'

'No! Not Richard!' Daisy was roused at last.

Joanne carefully did not look at her friend. There was something revealing about that involuntary exclamation and she wondered idly what the pleasant if serious-minded young student had done to offend Daisy. He had been used to lounging about the flat as though it was his second home. Being Joanne, she had not commented on his absence during the last few weeks.

'Not Richard . . . right.' She crossed his name from the list. 'Anyone else you'd like to ask?'

Daisy shrugged. 'Patti.'

Joanne had meant in the male line. But she said nothing. She wrote down Patti's name and added a couple more. 'I might ask David Montgomery,' she mused. 'You don't know him, do you? He took over from Lester Thorn as Professor Wilmot's Registrar. I met him at that party last week and rather liked him.' She did not think it necessary to mention that he also happened to be one of Gavin Fletcher's friends and might be persuaded to bring the man to the party.

She might not approve too much of Daisy's interest in him. She might not feel that he was likely to be serious or lasting in his pursuit of any woman. But she could not bear to go on seeing that misery in her friend's eyes. Daisy was eating her heart out over something . . . and it could be Gavin Fletcher. It was sometimes better to have something to remember of a man than never to know him at all, Joanne felt, quite unaware of how rapidly that relationship had developed and how abruptly it had ended.

Gavin Fletcher might just have lost interest, of course. Men did, very quickly. Daisy was a dear, but she did take things seriously and most men shied instinctively from intensity when they were only looking for light-hearted and short-lived adventure.

There was no harm in inviting someone to a party and Daisy might be pleased if Gavin Fletcher turned up. If she wanted him it was up to her to make a move in the right direction, Joanne felt. Even the shyest and most inexperienced of girls knew just how to reach out for what she wanted if she cared enough!

And if she was mistaken and Daisy was not interested, well, Joanne was beginning to wonder about a man who was reputed to be so attractive and so dangerous and she was rather looking forward to meeting him . . .

Daisy was not at all inclined for a party. She had been depressed for days. She knew it was very silly to allow a man she scarcely knew to make her so miserable—and even more foolish to be so sure that she loved him. But the feeling was deep and persistent and she could not shake it off.

It seemed that he had really made up his mind to put

her out of his life. For days, he had been ignoring her as though she did not exist except as a robot nurse in cap and apron, part of the ward furniture, just as in the days before he had so unexpectedly fulfilled her absurd dream and taken that brief, disturbing interest in her which had only succeeded in turning her entire world upside down!

Perhaps he was trying to protect her from possible heartache. He did not know that it was much too late, after all. Or perhaps he was anxious to protect himself from the demands of her unwelcome love for him. But it seemed a very drastic and unnecessary end to friendship, Daisy thought sadly, knowing very well that she could not have been content with mere friendship when she had known the near-ecstasy of his ardent lovemaking.

In her worst moments, she decided that he was punishing her for leading him on and then abruptly disappointing him.

At other times, not very much better, she was convinced that he had ceased to bother with her because she really was as unimportant to him as all the other girls he had lightly and carelessly loved.

At all times, she lived with the brutal candour of his declaration that he would never love her or wish to marry her, and Daisy, loving him with all the passion of her youthful and very trusting heart, could not believe that she would ever want to marry anyone else.

But there was very little point in fretting and regretting that he had finally turned his back on a girl who could not say anything but no!

'Can I leave the food to you, Daisy?' The list completed, Joanne glanced at the clock and suddenly realised that she had dawdled too long over lunch. 'I must dash! John and I will look after the drinks. It won't cost much as most people will bring bottles, I should think.'

Daisy was off duty. She had meant to have a lazy afternoon, writing letters, doing her nails. Now it seemed that she would have to shop for food and spend hours preparing rolls and sandwiches, sausage rolls and vol-au-vents and cheese straws.

'Yes, all right. I'll organise something,' she said, rather reluctantly.

Joanne smiled at her, slipping her arms into a long and fashionable cardigan and reaching for her shoulder bag. 'I expect you'll enjoy a party,' she said with her usual optimism. 'We haven't had one for ages!'

Daisy relented. Joanne meant well, she knew, suspecting that her friend thought she needed cheering. Well, she had not been the brightest or easiest of flat-mates just lately and Joanne had been very patient, very understanding. 'Sorry. I'm just being a drear,' she said, contrite. 'Of course I'll see to the food. We shall need plenty, I suppose. How many are you asking?'

'Oh, these things tend to snowball, don't they,' Joanne said airily. 'Cater for ten or twelve.'

'That means twenty,' Daisy returned, smiling. She knew Joanne's haphazard invitations to all and sundry! 'Heaven knows how we shall have room for them all!'

Joanne laughed. 'I know! But we always do, after all. It's the intimate atmosphere that makes our parties so popular, I think, sitting on each other's laps and being squeezed into corners with complete strangers makes for getting to know each other in no time at all!'

Daisy sat for a while over the remains of the light lunch they had shared. She knew there was much to be done, but her spirits did lift just a little at the thought of a party and a lively crowd of people.

She told herself firmly that she must stop moping for a man who no longer wanted her. It was absurd to feel that his going had left a terrible void in her life when they had known each other for such a little time.

But she missed him. She had liked the smile in his eyes, the way her heart lifted to him . . . and how could she ever forget the warmth of his lips or the eagerness of his body pressed against her own?

She sighed, knowing she must try to forget. Or she might end up with nothing in life but nursing and Hart-lake and the risk of turning into an embittered, sharp-tongued old maid like the legendary Sister Booth.

The flat swarmed with people that evening. Joanne's parties were always popular and no one refused an invitation and some guests brought friends in the conviction that they would be welcome. The more the merrier was Joanne's motto!

Daisy was thankful that she had been so busy all afternoon when she saw how rapidly the plates of food went the rounds and returned empty. Experience had taught her how to cater for hungry members of the medical profession and she went into the kitchen to do some more rolls and to bring out the vol-au-vents that she had kept back for just this kind of emergency.

She was pleased that the party was going so well. She felt a little like a wet blanket and was trying hard not to let it show. She did not lack for attention, but somehow there wasn't anyone who interested her among the many guests. The men who hovered about her were friendly and amusing and inclined to be amorous. Daisy sus-pected that they had heard rumours about her recently and were trying out their own theories on her likely response to overtures. She was not encouraging.

A noisy cheer announced the arrival of some late-comers. Daisy wondered wryly if the walls could stretch to accommodate any more people. They had already overflowed into the bedroom and the tiny kitchen and out on to the stairs. Wisely, they had invited those of their neighbours who were not on duty or busy with other engagements.

She squeezed past a couple in close embrace, gazing soulfully into each other's eyes. Someone took the plate of rolls from her hand with a glad cry. Someone else reached for the vol-au-vents,

The room was crowded and rather stuffy. Some couples were trying to dance, moving in a slow shuffle to the record on the stereo. Its loud beat, the talk and the laughter was overwhelming. Daisy could not see through the crush of people to the corner where Joanne was holding court. She was not particularly interested in the newcomers. She did not expect to know them for it had turned into that kind of party.

Patti was banging the back of a friend who had choked on a crumb of sausage roll and Daisy nodded in reply to the urgent request for water. As she turned back to the kitchen door, she heard Joanne call her above the tumult. Without glancing back, she raised a hand to show that she had heard and pushed between a couple who were furiously arguing the merits and demerits of a new group on the music scene.

Running the tap and rinsing a glass, Daisy did not look round as someone followed her into the small kitchen. She filled the glass with cold water to take to Patti's friend and turned—and the wet glass slipped from sud-

denly nerveless fingers as she found herself face to face
with Gavin.

A loud cheer went up at the sound of breaking glass.
Daisy scarcely noticed. She stared at Gavin, so unexpected and causing her heart to leap into her throat in
mingled delight and alarm that she might betray how
glad she was to see him.

'Hallo,' he said, not quite smiling. He had not expected to feel it like a blow to the solar plexus when she
turned her small, pretty, startled face to him. 'I seem to
have surprised you.'

Daisy found her voice with an effort. 'I didn't expect
you.'

'You didn't invite me.' A smile flickered. Then he
turned to the door to hold back the curious who were
crowding forward to discover the cause of the breakage.
'Will everyone please keep out for a few minutes while
we clear up the mess,' he said in his crisp, authoritative
way, very familiar on the ward but unlike the lazy,
attractive drawl that he used off duty. 'We don't want
any further accidents!'

Daisy had already reached for dustpan and brush and
cloth to clear up the broken glass. She was glad to have
something to do in those first difficult moments. She
wished she knew if he had come to the party because he
wanted to see her, or if he had come with one of the
many girls among the guests.

Gavin bent down to help, to retrieve the larger pieces.
She busied herself in reaching for the splinters of glass
that had in usual fashion scattered to all the most
inaccessible corners. Her heart was beating very fast and
she was much too conscious of him, very careful not to
meet his eyes or to brush by chance against his hand.

'Perhaps I don't come high on your list of friends to invite to a party,' he said lightly. 'You've been avoiding me, Daisy.'

She looked at him then, quickly, defensively, a little indignant. 'Boot on the other foot, I think!'

Gavin thought how lovely she was with that soft flush in her cheeks, her eyes bright with a kind of defiance. Her long hair was caught into a cluster of soft curls on the nape of her neck and she wore a long, multi-coloured evening skirt with a filmy black blouse that enhanced the fairness of hair and skin. She was very feminine, very pretty, quite enchanting.

He saw that she was wearing the gold chain that he had given her, the tilting gold heart nestling in the hollow of her throat with the *No* side uppermost. A wry smile quirked his lips as he wondered if he had expected anything else. But she still wore his present. Because she liked it, or because she still liked him, he wondered ruefully.

His arms still ached to hold her and his body stirred with the wanting that she could evoke so swiftly and so strongly. He resisted the temptation to kiss her, reminding himself that he had decided to keep out of her life for the very best of reasons. But he had been unable to resist the impulse to snatch just a few moments with her, away from the crowd.

Patti opened the kitchen door, looked in. 'Don't bother with the water, after all. Gareth just choked to death,' she said brightly, teasing. She checked in a little surprise at sight of Gavin. But she bravely stifled the impulse to exclaim. 'Hallo,' she said easily, smiling at him. 'Nice to see you.' She made it sound as though it was the most natural thing in the world for such an exalted personage as Sir Leonard's registrar to turn up at one of Joanne's wild parties.

She made way for Joanne at a light touch on her arm. 'Do we have any more sandwiches, Daisy? We seem to be feeding the five thousand!' Joanne smiled warmly at Gavin. It was part apology for intruding, part appreciation of his good looks. Joanne was rather susceptible to tall, dark and very attractive men.

'Sorry. We've run out of bread, I'm afraid.' Daisy's heart sank as she saw that exchange of smiles, the hint of invitation in Joanne's eyes and the undeniable response in the way that Gavin looked at her beautiful friend. She had always known that she would be cast into shadow once he met Joanne—but being prepared did not make it any easier!

'Oh! Well, the hungry hordes will just have to keep going on crisps and peanuts,' Joanne said lightly. She glanced again at Gavin with that warm, coquettish interest in her eyes. 'You don't seem to have a drink, Gavin. Daisy, if you don't look after a very attractive man then you must expect to lose him, you know!' The words were light, laughing, but with quite unmistakable meaning.

Gavin smiled, recognising the lure in eyes and voice. They had been introduced that afternoon by David Montgomery. He was too much of a man to be blind to the rich and alluring beauty of Joanne Laidlaw and he had known instinctively that she would not be averse to a little light-hearted flirtation. He knew from past experience that the only way to put one woman out of his mind was to concentrate on the attractions of another.

Joanne was a very different girl to Daisy. She was a lively charmer, obviously well-versed in the art of flirta-

tion. She would not take him seriously and it might serve
his present purpose to pretend an interest in the girl.
Perhaps it would hurt Daisy, but it might protect her
from future heartache. If he gave her good reason to
despise him, she might soon forget that she had ever
been inclined to like him too much. In fact, Gavin
thought wryly, she might forget all about him long
before he could forget her. There was something very
memorable about the enchanting and innocent
Daisy . . .

He put an arm about Joanne's slender waist and
smiled into the beautiful, challenging eyes. 'I daresay
you know just how to look after a man,' he drawled with
the particularly seductive note in his deep voice that
drew the women like a magnet.

Joanne smiled up at him. 'Try me . . . !' Her tone was
teasing, but with an underlying provocation that no man
could mistake.

Daisy shot the broken glass from the dustpan into an
empty cardboard box, feeling just as though all her
foolish hopes and dreams went with it. She was not blind
or deaf to that invitation and response. She was about to
lose him to Joanne—and it was entirely her own fault.
She had snubbed him, rebuffed him and possibly even
hurt him. It was very little comfort to know that she
would have lost him eventually, anyway.

She supposed she ought to be thankful that she still
had her virginity, even if he had taken her heart. But she
was not. She foolishly persisted in grieving for the
ecstatic miracle of delight that she had been so near to
knowing in his arms and could have cherished as a very
precious memory, a golden moment in her life. Now she
would never have another opportunity to say yes or no to

him, she realised. For he would be too involved with her beautiful friend to have any time for her.

Joanne drifted thoughtfully back to the party.

She thought that Daisy seemed annoyed rather than pleased that Gavin Fletcher had sought her out within minutes of his arrival at the party. He seemed to be still sufficiently interested to go on trying. Joanne decided that he was not getting anywhere. She had sensed the hint of frustration in his mood that had urged him to take her up on that not-so-subtle invitation.

She supposed that Daisy knew what she was doing. If she wanted the man then she could obviously have him for the mere lift of a finger. But perhaps she really did not want him at all. Perhaps she was fretting over the curiously absent Richard rather than the very attractive registrar. Joanne discovered that she was hoping that Daisy did not want him—because she rather thought that *she* did!

'I met your elusive friend at last, you see,' Gavin said lightly.

'I'm surprised that she escaped your attention until now.' Daisy tried to speak lightly, as though she did not care that he had suddenly become aware of Joanne's attractions. 'I thought you had a list of all the good-looking girls at Hartlake and were gradually working your way through them.'

He chuckled. 'That's true. But they are all nurses. Physiotherapists don't come in my way very often.' He hesitated and then added lightly: 'I know you don't approve of me, Daisy. But a man can't help the way he's made, you know.'

'You don't have to explain yourself to me. I don't care what you do.' She began to clear away some of the empty bottles and dirty glasses and half eaten food that littered the kitchen, needing to be busy and hoping that her tone had been convincing.

'You seem to be maid of all work,' Gavin said. 'Don't you ever get to the ball, Cinderella?'

She ran hot water into the bowl to wash up the glasses and crockery. She was not naive enough to hope that his words were the forerunner to an invitation. She knew that she would not be dancing in his arms at Founder's Ball at the end of the week.

'Sometimes . . .' She looked at him with a slight smile. Her heart might be breaking but she did not have to let him know it, she told herself sternly. 'I shall be there on Saturday with all the other Cinderellas.'

A wry smile quirked his lips. Her tone told him unmistakably that she was not expecting his escort. He did not doubt that she had made arrangements to go with someone else. She had been friendly for months with one of the medical students. The man might not be very important to her, but his attentions and interest were probably soothing to her wounded pride. He had left it very late to make his own arrangements. Perhaps he had been hoping to take Daisy. He seemed to have had a great many of his hopes dashed where she was concerned he thought ruefully.

'Looking for Prince Charming?' he teased gently.

Daisy stiffened. She supposed she did seem very young and foolishly sentimental to him, she thought bitterly. 'Perhaps,' she said lightly.

'Well, you deserve to find him, girl . . .'

Daisy's hands rinsed glasses as though her life depended on it. She was suddenly very near to tears. It was just as well that he obviously did not know that she had

ceased to look for the love of her life when she first saw
him on the ward. But it hurt that he could be so blind, so
insensitive—and so utterly indifferent.

As he went from the kitchen, she did not turn round,
call him back. There had been careless dismissal in his
words. She knew that he had gone in search of Joanne
. . . clever, confident Joanne who knew better than to
fall in love and break her heart. Joanne was his kind of
girl, after all . . .

It was some time before she steeled herself to go into
the other room, only to be seized upon by a very drunk
acquaintance who insisted that she dance with him.
There was scarcely room to breathe let alone dance, but
Daisy shuffled obligingly in his arms, trying not to mind
his closeness or his beer-laden breath.

She saw that Joanne was making headway with Gavin.
With her arms linked about his neck, they were moving
to the music, but no one could call it dancing, Daisy
thought painfully.

She had liked other men in the past who had left her
for Joanne, drawn by the vibrant beauty and the warm
personality and the more exciting promise of her friend.
They had never really mattered very much, of course,
but Gavin did . . .

CHAPTER ELEVEN

THE party did not fizzle out until the early hours. Some of the noisier elements were persuaded to depart soon after midnight and most of the casual guests gradually drifted away. At last only close friends were left to settle into chairs or on cushions on the floor, talking quietly, listening to music, arms about each other.

Daisy sat with John Seymour, smiling and friendly and even managing to be slightly provocative, feeling absolutely dead inside. She longed for the party to end so that she could go to bed and try to blot out the too-vivid picture of Gavin and Joanne, his arm about her, his long fingers lightly stroking the smooth cheek, the slender throat, the nape of her neck and the glorious chestnut hair as they talked in low, intimate murmurs.

He behaved like a potential lover and Joanne was encouraging him, making no secret of her liking and interest and willingness for more than casual friendship. She was not a promiscuous girl by any means, but she enjoyed playing with fire—and it would amuse her to give the grapevine something to talk about, Daisy thought ruefully.

They would not make any serious demands on each other, of course, and that would suit them both. Joanne would not expect him to love her or to be loyal and she would certainly not be foolish enough to weave romantic dreams about him or to fall in love.

Daisy tumbled into bed when everyone had finally

left, not even bothering to brush her long hair. She pulled the covers firmly about her neck and hoped that Joanne would not rub salt in the wound by talking about the evening. She had never felt so wretched or so bereft in her life and she was having trouble in keeping back the tears.

She throbbed with pain and longing and utter despair. She did not blame Joanne for holding out her arms to someone as attractive and as exciting as Gavin. But it was a very bitter blow that he had gone so readily into those arms. She wondered wearily what else she had expected. Wasn't any woman much the same to a man like Gavin? Disappointed by one, it was inevitable that he had promptly looked around for another, like the heartless and sensual rake that he was.

Daisy knew she was a fool to shed such hot and painful tears for such a man. She knew, too, that she loved him with all her heart . . .

Joanne glanced uncertainly at the mound beneath the blankets. The best part of an evening was to talk it over, no matter how late it might be. Daisy was usually eager and willing to do so. It was not like her to settle down so quickly for sleep that it seemed like defensive action.

Joanne wondered if Daisy had enjoyed the party at all. She had certainly taken very little notice of Gavin Fletcher and Joanne was rather relieved about that. It was not part of her code for living that she deliberately reached out for another girl's man. She liked him, found him attractive, and thought she could enjoy a few weeks of flirtation with him as long as it did not hurt or upset Daisy.

But Daisy had seemed indifferent, quite untroubled by his attentions to another girl—which might be disinterest and might just as easily be pride! Joanne wished she knew.

She might have ceased to worry and begun to look forward to seeing the attractive registrar again if it was not for a niggling little doubt.

Daisy had flirted with John Seymour—and Daisy never flirted. It was alien to her nature and she was not very good at light-hearted coquetry. But she had certainly done her best to flirt with John who had obliged her with smiling good nature once he found that Joanne's attention was taken up by another man.

Joanne and John were friends, fond of each other without commitment, and she did not mind that he had been so nice to Daisy. She was not jealous. She was just puzzled. For it was not like Daisy to parade an ability to attract and she could not help wondering if the whole performance had been carefully staged.

She ran a brush through her hair. 'I'm glad that Gavin Fletcher turned up,' she said lightly. 'I didn't really think he would.' Daisy grunted. Joanne hesitated. 'He's very attractive, isn't he? Of course, you know him better than I do, but he does seem rather nice.' Daisy turned over and pointedly drew the covers over her head. 'I don't want to tread on your toes, love,' Joanne went on. 'Are you sure you don't want him?'

Daisy sat up suddenly, pummelled the pillows to relieve her feelings. 'He isn't mine to give away.' She was very careful to keep all trace of emotion from her tone.

'I think he could be,' Joanne said, smiling.

'Oh, rubbish! He just makes a pass at every girl. It doesn't mean a thing.' Daisy looked pointedly at the clock beside the bed. 'I wish you'd stop talking about

Gavin Fletcher and let me sleep, Joanne,' she suddenly snapped as a new wave of misery swept over her. 'Some people have to work tomorrow!'

'Sorry!'

Daisy put her head in her hands. 'Oh, so am I!' Her voice was muffled. 'I didn't mean to snap. But I'm so tense and irritable these days. I don't know what's the matter with me!'

'Nothing so uncomplicated as pre-menstrual tension, I daresay,' Joanne said, rather dryly. She put down her brush, looked at Daisy as she impatiently thrust the mass of pale hair from her face. 'It is Gavin, isn't it?'

'No. I don't even like him. He's selfish and conceited and . . .' She broke off, biting her lip.

'And I made things worse.'

Daisy sighed. 'No. You didn't do anything. He was just trying to show me that I don't matter very much. That's the kind of man he is. Any woman suits his purpose.' Her tone was heavy rather than scathing.

Joanne raised an eyebrow. She did not think she was flattered to be told so bluntly that a man had only been using her to his own ends rather than taking a genuine interest.

'Weren't you showing him that he doesn't matter when you were playing up to John?' she asked, amused.

'He doesn't matter!'

'Then you won't mind if he takes me to the Ball on Saturday?'

Daisy minded very much, but she did not mean to say so. Besides, she had been expecting it. It had been stupid to dream of dancing in his arms, of everything miraculously coming right on that special night of the year. Dreams did not come true, after all.

'Of course not,' she said stoutly.

Joanne studied her thoughtfully. 'I can tell him that I've changed my mind, you know. I like him, but there are lots of men I like just as well,' she said with truth.

Daisy did not doubt that Joanne could take her pick from a dozen escorts. It did not really matter that she had no escort. She did not want to go with anyone but Gavin—and if he was to be there with Joanne on his arm then she did not want to go at all!

'There are lots of men I like very much better,' she said firmly, lying in her teeth.

Joanne felt torn. She was interested in Gavin Fletcher, but she did not want to hurt Daisy. Nothing shattered friendship between two girls faster than both wanting the same man, she knew. But with Daisy insisting that she was not impressed she was tempted to ignore that little doubt, that little uneasiness.

For Daisy was not a child. She ought to know her own mind, and she was much too sensible to risk her happiness for the sake of pride. Perhaps she had good reason to snub Gavin. Perhaps her impatience stemmed from everyone's readiness to believe that they were involved with each other. Perhaps the grapevine gossip had interfered with her relationship with Richard and that had made her unhappy.

It might even be that Gavin had started the rumour about himself and Daisy to turn Richard against her and leave the way clear for his own hopes. If it was so, then it would be doing Daisy a favour if she whisked him away and gave the gossips something else to talk about and allowed the lovers to get together again, Joanne decided with her usual lively optimism.

She hoped that her friendship with Gavin would not

hurt Daisy, anyway. That little doubt did persist. But she could not help feeling that it was an essential part of growing up that one learned to take one's chance of happiness or heartache in life.

Opportunity offered and should be seized with both hands—or it was lost!

Daisy was grateful that she was not on duty until one-thirty. She slept late and then helped Joanne to tidy the flat after the party. Neither of them mentioned Gavin Fletcher.

To her relief, she found that Sister Sweet was off for the afternoon. Trish King was in charge of the ward. She would not work them into the ground as long as the routine chores were done.

Daisy was very tired. She had hardly slept, hugging her hurt and knowing bitterly that it was her own fault that Gavin had slipped through her hands and into Joanne's eager arms.

If she had not been such a coward, so afraid of loving when it was already too late for choice in the matter, she might be looking forward to going to the Ball with him.

Perhaps he would have tired of her very soon as she had feared. But at least she might have had some golden memories to treasure. As it was, she had nothing to look forward to but the hard work and routine and doubtful satisfaction of a nursing career when she yearned for husband, home and children—and nothing to look back on but a stupid reluctance to prove to a man that she loved him.

He might have found something in her arms that no other girl had given him, after all, she thought wistfully. He might even have loved her one day. There had been liking and affection and even the warmth of tenderness in his attitude to her until she had earned his contempt with her refusal to face up to the basic facts of living and loving.

But it was too late for regrets. He had ceased to want her and with the advent of Joanne into his life he would soon forget that she even existed!

Gavin walked into the ward, looking for Sister or Staff Nurse King. The curtains were drawn about one of the beds. Daisy was the only nurse in sight, standing at the foot of a patient's bed with arms crossed, enjoying a few minutes of relaxed chat.

Catching her eye, he beckoned.

Daisy hesitated. Trish was busy in the closed cubicle. Everyone else was temporarily off the ward. It seemed that she would have to attend to him and she really would rather not.

'Nurse!' His tone was rather peremptory. Senior doctors were not kept waiting while a junior nurse made up her mind whether to answer a summons.

Daisy lingered to straighten the patient's coverlet and to retrieve a magazine that had fallen to the floor, hoping that Trish or someone else would appear and rescue her from the necessity of speaking to him.

'You'd better see what he wants, Nurse,' the patient suggested with a twinkle in his eyes. 'He looks a bit annoyed to me.'

Daisy glanced at him reluctantly. 'Yes, I suppose so.'

Gavin had taken his stethoscope from his coat pocket and he was flicking the rubber tubing lightly against his wrist. It was an unconscious habit, born of irritation. He watched her walk down the ward, not hurrying, and he was suddenly very angry with her obvious reluctance to have anything to do with him, either personally or in the course of her work. If she was sulking because he had turned his attentions to her more responsive friend then she had only herself to blame, he thought impatiently. He had been more than willing to devote himself to her. He might even have given up the sensual pursuit of a variety of women for her sake . . .

'Don't keep me waiting another time, Nurse!' he snapped coldly as she reached him. 'It might be a matter of life or death!'

Her chin tilted. 'And is it?' she demanded, disliking his tone. Perhaps he did despise her these days, but there was no need for him to snarl at her in front of the patients.

He quelled her with an angry glance. 'Where's Sister?'

'Off duty. Staff Nurse King is in charge, but she's very busy.' She indicated the drawn curtains about the bed. 'What is it? Can I help?' There was a hint of reluctance in the offer.

'No. You aren't qualified, are you?' He did not mean to be curt. But he was in a hurry and she had already caused him to lose valuable time. He knew that she had deliberately kept him waiting. He did not realise that his summons had been arrogant or that she had reacted very strongly to his appearance on the ward.

He had a clinic full of patients waiting for him and a testy Sir Leonard demanding to know why his usually efficient registrar had failed to carry out a simple instruction. Perhaps he was also rather annoyed that Daisy persisted in haunting his thoughts and interfering with his concentration on his work. It had never happened before and he was not sure that he welcomed the impact of this particular girl on his life. There seemed to be very little future in wanting her, anyway.

'What is it you want?'

'I'm going to draw some fluid from Mr Hunter's pleural cavity. I need assistance, but you're too inexperienced to be any good to me, I'm afraid.'

She flushed, believing he had chosen his words deliberately. 'And you don't mean to let me forget it, do you! I'm sorry I'm such a disappointment in so many ways,' she said tartly.

Gavin's mouth tightened abruptly. He looked at her with a spark of anger in his dark eyes. 'Damn you, Daisy! Don't bring personalities into it!' He knew a spurt of disappointment that she was as human as the next girl, after all. It seemed that he had begun to invest her with too many good qualities, he thought dryly. 'Right now I'm a very busy doctor and you're just another nurse. I haven't time to quarrel with you. Just go and tell your staff nurse that I need her to assist me.'

'Tell her yourself!' Tired and tense, past caring for the niceties of hospital etiquette, Daisy flared in sudden resentment of the arrogance and autocracy of his manner, so like the more insufferable consultants of the old school and so unexpected in a man who was noted for his charm and courtesy to staff and patients alike. She no longer merited either, it seemed! 'I'm sick of being treated like a servant by doctors who think they are gods!'

Gavin stiffened, furious.

Patients turned their heads or sat up in beds, delighted with the unexpected excitement in a long and tedious day that was broken only by the routine rounds, predictable meals and too-brief visiting hours.

Trish, attracted by raised voices, came out to see what was going on, and took in the situation at a glance.

'That's quite enough, Nurse,' she admonished Daisy in low, shocked tones. 'Leave the ward until you are in more control of yourself!'

Under a barrage of mostly curious and some sympathetic eyes, Daisy fled. She sought refuge in the small room where the juniors kept their cloaks and caps and clean aprons and snatched a few moments for a cup of coffee during the long hours of duty.

She sank into a chair and put her head on the table and cried, quite convinced that this time she would be sent to Matron and sacked and would have to leave Hartlake, her nursing career at an abrupt end. She had committed the unforgivable sin.

She had flown at him like a virago—and a junior never, *never* answered back to a senior nurse or doctor, no matter what the provocation. It upset the patients and undermined authority and morale. That had been drummed into her enough in P.T.S.

Well, she would never see Gavin again. And as she hated him for speaking to her in that beastly way and looking at her as though she was dirt, she did not care if she never saw him again! And if she never saw him again she might as well be dead!

Utterly wretched, Daisy sobbed.

Trish put her head briefly into the room. She cast her eyes to heaven and hurried away to assist the registrar with his patient. For the girl's sake, she was glad that Sarah Sweet was off duty. Faced by a furious registrar and a busily speculating ward, she would not have hesitated to suspend the junior just as she had done before, and it was doubtful if she would have relented a second time about sending her to Matron.

Trish was justifiably annoyed that the fresh contretemps between Daisy and the doctor should have happened while she was in charge of the ward. Such things reflected so badly on her management. She asked little of the staff except that the work be done and the ward run smoothly and they did not usually let her down.

She supposed reluctantly that she would have to mention the incident to Sister . . .

Patti was sent by a ruffled staff nurse to comfort her friend. She put an arm about Daisy's heaving shoulders and her heart went out to the girl who had made the age-old mistake of falling in love with the wrong man. She had heard stories about Gavin Fletcher that were enough to make a girl's hair curl, she thought wryly. Probably highly exaggerated for the most part, but with enough truth in them to make a level-headed girl like Daisy steer clear of him if she had not woven dreams about him long before she even knew him. Dreaming was a very dangerous pastime.

Needing to confide in someone and quite unable to admit to a personally involved Joanne that she was hopelessly in love with Gavin, Daisy found herself pouring some of it out to the sympathetic first-year nurse.

'Well, I do feel for you,' Patti said with truth. Daisy's misery stirred memories that she preferred to keep hidden in her heart and mind. 'But there isn't much you can do but grin and bear it and try to forget your feelings in a lot of hard work. You can't force a man to care about you.' Privately she felt that Gavin Fletcher did care, but she knew better than to raise the girl's hopes by saying so. Love had to find its own way out of the maze of misunderstanding—or die in the attempt.

'I wish I didn't see so much of him,' Daisy said unhappily, splashing cold water over her flushed face and hot eyes. 'It doesn't help. I'm sure he knows how miserable I am—and just doesn't care!'

Patti reserved her judgment. It did not seem to her that he was so indifferent to Daisy's feelings—and surely he made more visits to the ward than was usual for a registrar who had a houseman to take care of much of the routine work?

'It doesn't hurt for ever,' she said gently, wondering if that was true. 'There are some really nice men in the world, you know. Don't let a good-looking charmer break your heart.'

Daisy was a little indignant with the casually dismissing description. She knew that there was so much more to Gavin. He could be kind and very thoughtful and tender. She would not love him so much if she did not like him so well, too.

She sighed. 'I wish I had some leave owing to me. I'd go home and try to put him out of my mind.'

'Absence only makes the heart grow fonder,' Patti quoted wryly. 'You'd dream about him and build him up into a perfect saint. Stick around and you'll realise that he isn't and never will be anything but a very ordinary man.'

Patti went back to her work and Daisy put on a clean apron and adjusted her cap, wondering if she would be allowed to return to the ward if she apologised to Trish.

She emerged into the corridor, heart beating rather fast, to find Trish and Gavin talking just outside the swing doors of the ward. She had hoped to find him gone. She was tempted to make a hasty retreat, but she had been noticed.

Rather pale, but with head high and eyes just a little defiant in case they met Gavin's, she walked towards them. Trish turned to her. 'It's time for rounds, Nurse,' she said as though nothing had happened. 'Please hurry. We seem to be all behind this afternoon.'

'Yes, of course, Staff. . .' She gave her senior a very grateful smile. No wonder everyone liked the staff nurse. She was so warm-hearted and understanding and good-natured. It was good of her to turn a blind eye. She might have a private word with her later, but at least she had not scolded her in front of Gavin.

She hurried into the ward, trying not to mind that Gavin had looked through her so coldly. Patti had given her some good advice and she must try to follow it. He was not the only man in the world, after all.

She threw herself into her work and refused to appear anything but cheerfully efficient. Whisking round the ward with Patti, tidying lockers and straightening beds and plumping pillows, she was thankful that her briskness dispelled the slyly amused curiosity of some of the patients who had witnessed that scene with Gavin.

Although they were short-staffed, Trish was able to write up her report at the end of the afternoon with the feeling that the impulsive junior had done her best to atone. Before leaving the ward, she called Daisy into the office and spoke to her, but very kindly.

'I don't know what quarrel you have with Dr Fletcher and I don't want to know,' she said gently. 'But you mustn't bring it to work with you, Nurse.'

'I know, Staff. I really am sorry.'

'You're doing your best to blot your copy book, aren't you?' Trish smiled wryly. 'You came to this ward with such a good report from Sister Percival. Your work is careful and caring and you get on well with patients. I know Sister is pleased with you. But you do seem to have trouble with your personal feelings. Perhaps it will be easier when you move to another ward.'

'Yes, Staff.' The hands demurely linked behind her back suddenly clenched at the thought of leaving Fleming. The frequent encounters with Gavin might not bring her anything but pain and trouble, but she needed desperately to go on seeing him.

Trish studied her thoughtfully. 'I know we can't do without them, but doctors are the bane of our existence,' she said lightly, relaxing formality. 'Particularly the good-looking ones. They cause havoc among the juniors and I've lost count of the times that I've found a first-year sobbing her heart out in the sluice because a houseman who smiled at her one day didn't seem to know she existed the next. Second-years have usually grown up enough to realise that their work and particularly the patients come before their off-duty affairs.'

Daisy said nothing. But she felt the gentle rebuke much more than any sharp scold by the more forceful Sister Sweet.

Trish began to collate the papers on her desk. 'All right, Nurse. We'll say no more about it. I don't think there's any need for me to mention the matter to Sister, do you? But don't let it happen again, there's a good girl.' She smiled, very warm.

'Thank you, Staff . . .'

Daisy was relieved to escape with so little said. Sister Sweet would have wiped the floor with her, she knew.

CHAPTER TWELVE

GAVIN returned to the ward later that evening. Daisy came out of the kitchen with a milk feed for a patient and saw him talking to Sister Sweet. Her heart jolted uncomfortably. She wondered if they were talking about that scene on the ward. Trish King had overlooked it. Sister would not, she knew.

As she supported the man who was too ill to do much for himself, encouraging him to take a little necessary nourishment, she glanced down the ward to where the registrar and the sister were standing, deep in conversation. They seemed to be discussing a patient. Gavin referred now and again to the thick case history in his hand. Sister left him briefly to take a chart from the foot of a patient's bed and returned to check one or two points with him.

Rather animated, she looked quite pretty. She had come back to the ward after her few hours off in an unusually mellow mood. Gavin was exercising his careless charm and getting the inevitable response too, Daisy thought dryly, and then admitted fairly that it was probably unconscious.

Oh, he knew well enough that he was a very attractive man with a potent charisma that got him almost every woman he wanted. It would be surprising if he did not know it! But Daisy did not think he was setting out to charm Sister Sweet that evening. He seemed more interested in the patient who was not responding to treatment.

She turned her attention back to her own patient. 'Just a little more, Mr Wade,' she coaxed as he feebly turned his head away from the feeding cup. Daisy wiped the man's mouth and the slow trickle of milk that was making its way down his chin and then eased him into a more comfortable position against her arm. 'Just one more mouthful, Mr Wade—and I shall be really pleased with you for doing so well!' She had to speak quite loudly to get through to him. He was really too ill for anything to register. He was resisting food now and it seemed that a houseman would have to be called to put up a drip to keep him alive.

Gavin looked in her direction, attracted by the sound of her voice. As their eyes met, he smiled, so warmly that her heart soared. It was so totally unexpected that she almost dropped the feeding cup. He had a positive talent for taking her by surprise, she thought, veiling her eyes in disconcerted haste.

How could a girl ever know where she was with such a man! Only a few hours before he had been damning her as though she was nothing but a nuisance in his life. Now he smiled at her as though she was something very special.

As she bent over the patient, doing her best to get just a little more of the feed into him, Daisy told herself that it was not really surprising that a man with Gavin's fatal fascination for women did not want to settle down or give up his enjoyable and obviously precious independence. Why should he bother to fall seriously in love with one woman when he could enjoy himself in light-hearted fashion with so many, sailing through life without the least heartache, his work and career unaffected by personal difficulty or despair?

Daisy envied his detachment. But men were so different to women in their basic attitudes to love and life. And doctors were a breed apart from most men, it seemed.

Medical students got into the way of working hard and playing hard in the very early days of their training. Long hours and concentrated study on the wards, in theatre or clinic, meant that they needed to relax at the end of the day. Young and virile men naturally chose to unwind in the company of a pretty girl and there were plenty to choose from in a big teaching hospital. Junior nurses, many of them from the provinces and some of them rather more interested in men than in medicine, were easily impressed by the air of confident sophistication and a certain glamour that most of the students donned with their white coats.

By the time a young doctor qualified, he was often disinclined for early marriage, having discovered and enjoyed all the advantages of eligible bachelorhood without celibacy.

In Gavin's case, working towards an early consultancy, it was very unlikely that he had any plans to marry for some years, if ever. So, like many men in his position, he avoided the risk of falling seriously in love. He enjoyed a variety of light-hearted affairs and extricated himself with masculine adroitness at the first hint of a deeper involvement than he desired. He was an expert at the game of love.

Daisy had been a novice. She realised that there had never been the slightest risk for him in their relationship. The thought of loving her had never entered his head.

She had only been another potential conquest to prove his sexual prowess. She was glad that she had resisted him, she told herself firmly.

She knew she should set about falling out of love with him as quickly as possible. There were plenty of other men in the world just as Patti had pointed out—and most of them were probably much more reliable and less likely to break her heart. So why should she be so sure that there was no one like Gavin, with his lazy, dancing smile and laughing dark eyes? Why was she stubbornly convinced that no other man in the world could quicken her pulses and flood her with that tingling desire as he did?

Oh, she was a fool! But how could she help loving a man who captivated her with his charm even while he was infuriating her with that confident belief that he had only to smile and she would forgive him everything?

Mr Wade had drifted into a semi-comatose state. Daisy had managed to persuade him to take half the feed by dribbling it gently into his mouth and coaxing him to swallow.

She made him comfortable, but he did not seem to be aware of any of her ministrations. Daisy went to report to Sister.

She waited, hands behind her back, eyes everywhere but running the risk of meeting Gavin's, until Sister decided to notice her. Gavin did not glance at her again.

At last, Sister nodded agreement and moved to return the patient's chart to the foot of the bed. 'What is it, Nurse? Mr Wade? Oh, yes.' She looked along the ward towards the sick man. 'Very well, Nurse. At least we've got some food into him for the moment. Perhaps you could try again before you go off duty.' She glanced at her watch. 'You may take your break now. We seem to be quiet and I mean to relax for ten minutes, too.'

'Yes, Sister. Thank you, Sister.' As always, it was a very automatic response. She left the ward, aware that Gavin watched her and wondering why he was still hanging about when his business with Sister seemed to be finished.

She washed the feeding cup and tidied the kitchen. Then she went across the corridor to the juniors' room to make herself some coffee. The kettle was just on the boil when Gavin walked in. Daisy glanced at him, startled. 'You aren't allowed in here,' she said quickly defensively. It was her response to him that she feared rather than anything he might say or do, as usual.

'I daresay I know the rules better than you do,' he drawled with his attractive smile. 'I've broken most of them in my time.'

'And caused a lot of trouble for the poor juniors who were daft enough to encourage you!'

'Some of them walked into it with their eyes wide open,' he declared, quite unrepentant. 'They aren't all as innocent as you, girl.' He pulled out a chair, sat down. 'Relax, love. It isn't the first time I've had a cup of coffee in the juniors' room. I haven't been shot for it yet.'

'*I* might be sacked for it,' she said, tart.

'Life would be very dull if we didn't take the occasional risk.' His dark eyes twinkled at her engagingly. 'Your first-year is scrubbing out the sluice. Pamela Mason is busy on the ward. Staff Nurse Grant is on special in a side ward and Sister is putting her feet up in the office. We won't be disturbed and I want to talk to you.'

'I don't think we've anything to say to each other,' she said firmly. But she reached for another mug. She pushed the coffee towards him, ruefully telling herself that she was an idiot to be disarmed by his smile, quickened by his presence in the room.

'Sit down, Daisy.'

She hesitated. But there was weariness rather than command in that quiet voice. She glanced at him. He did look tired, rather tense. Foolishly she felt like putting her arms about him, drawing that dark head to her breast.

She drew a chair to the table and sat down as far from him as possible, resisting temptation. She saw the familiar amusement flicker in his dark eyes and felt that he was laughing at her youthful immaturity and apprehension.

She waited for him to speak. He was silent for so long that she began to fidget, toying with a spoon, stirring her coffee unnecessarily. She felt his eyes on her face but she refused to look at him.

'What do you want, Gavin?' she asked at last, a trifle impatiently. 'What is there to talk about?'

'You and me,' he suggested quietly. 'Us.'

Her heart jumped at the linking. But she had seen the way he looked at Joanne—the way that a man like him would always look at women. Surely he was not trying to say that he still wanted her despite everything!

It could only be masculine refusal to admit defeat. Let her once surrender and he would walk away for ever, thinking as little of her as he did of every woman who gave him what he wanted. Daisy knew it in her heart, in her blood, in her weak and very tempted body.

'There isn't any us,' she said, very cool, forcing herself to say it. 'Not now and not ever.'

He would go away and she would be sorry. But in her

heart she would know that she had done the right thing, however much it hurt. Loving a man liké Gavin belonged to a dream in which he loved her, too. Reality was something very different, she thought sadly.

Gavin looked at her, his heart thudding. There was a fierce obstinacy in him that insisted on wanting her—and a very real fear that he might be mistaken in thinking that she wanted him, too. Not just for now, but always, despite those determined words.

He needed to take her into his arms and hold her very close. He was urged to admit to loving at last, knowing that he ought not to lose out on her warmth and sweetness and enchantment.

He had never been at a loss in his pursuit of a woman. He had always known exactly what to say or do to secure what he wanted. He had a wealth of experience on which to draw. But no woman had ever been as important as Daisy. He was desperately afraid of saying or doing the wrong thing. What was the right thing where she was concerned. He was damned if he knew! He had tried so many times and in so many ways—and got nowhere!

'Joanne isn't important, you know,' he said, reaching to take her hand.

Daisy moved from his touch, very pointedly. 'None of us are,' she said brightly before he could say more. 'We're just names on a list.'

Until now, Gavin had enjoyed the reputation that he had built up so carefully through the years. It had amused him to scandalise the prudes and shake the fuddy-duddies and stir up the grapevine gossips. He was a very good doctor and his work spoke for itself, and he had always taken care to keep just inside the limits that were set for any member of the medical profession. But they had been good, exciting years.

Now, he did regret it, very much. For Daisy might never believe that he cared more for her than for anything else in the world—including his work! She might never trust him enough to love him. But he had to try.

'You're different, Daisy,' he said, a little wryly. For it was not easy for a proudly independent man with all his experience to admit that a stubborn little second-year nurse had brought him to his knees in humble loving.

She smiled, brittle. 'I know. I keep saying no,' she returned lightly. 'That's what makes me different, isn't it? Men like a challenge, don't they—and you're so conceited that you won't accept that I'm just not interested.'

Gavin thrust both hands through his thick black curls in a strangely despairing gesture. 'I expect it seems like conceit,' he admitted. 'It isn't. It's concern. I don't want to believe that you aren't open to persuasion.' He leaned forward to look deep into the defiant blue eyes. 'I've fallen in love with you, girl.'

Her heart stopped.

Perhaps hearts didn't really stop for such reasons or soar to great heights—or even come near to breaking in two. But just lately her heart seemed to be doing all manner of odd things!

How many, many times she had heard him say just those words to her in a dream! How wonderful it had always been to hear them spoken with their magical promise of almost unbearable happiness! How very different was the reality.

Because she could not believe him.

He did not behave like a man in love, she thought bleakly, remembering that he had been able to ignore her for days, remembering that he had made light love to Joanne without any thought for her feelings, remembering how he had looked and spoken only that afternoon as though he thoroughly disliked and despised her.

No, she did not believe him.

'Daisy . . .' His tone was very gentle. He touched his hand to her soft cheek in a light, seeking caress.

Daisy steeled her heart, her melting body. 'There goes the last illusion,' she said brightly. 'That was one gambit you hadn't tried and I was fool enough to believe that you never would. I thought you had integrity if nothing else. I guess I was wrong.' She got up and took her untouched coffee to the small sink and poured it down the drain, and with it went the foolish fancy that she loved him, she told herself firmly. The dream had finally come to its very predictable end.

Gavin rose. He moved to catch her by the shoulders, to swing her round to face him. Dark eyes blazing, he ignored the instinctive murmur of protest at his bruising grip on her soft flesh. 'Bitch!' he said, angry. He kissed her, hard.

Daisy slapped him.

'Oh, hell!' he said furiously, cursing the temper that was as hard to control as his ardour at times. 'I'm sorry, love. You know I didn't mean it.' He tried to draw her into his arms, to kiss her in love instead of anger.

Daisy resisted fiercely. 'You never mean anything. That's just the trouble!'

'I love you. I do mean that,' he told her, very tense.

He had never said the words to any woman before. He had never expected to mean them quite so much and he found them rather hard to say. Perhaps that was due to the militant light in those vivid eyes and the angry tilt to her chin. Perhaps they would have been better left unsaid just now.

Wrong time, wrong place, he thought wryly, regretting the tension and the need that had brought him back to the ward so determined to talk to her and try to put things right between them.

Daisy's resolution wavered as she saw the warm glow in his dark eyes. It was oddly convincing. Then she thought of all the uncertainty, all the unhappiness, all the problems that had come from being too eager to believe that he meant what he said.

'Will you please get out of my life and stay out,' she said angrily. On a sudden impulse, she fumbled for the chain that had never left her neck since he put it there. Unfastening it with trembling fingers, she threw it down on the table. His eyes narrowed abruptly. 'I don't want you or anything to do with you!' She stalked from the room with a desperate need to escape before the look in his eyes broke down all her defences.

Two minutes later, she rushed back, heart beating wildly, to retrieve the little gold heart on its slender gold chain that meant so much to her. For she had regretted the impulse as soon as she carried it out.

The necklace had gone—and so had Gavin.

Crossing Main Hall on her way home that night after a seemingly never-ending spell of duty, Daisy saw Richard for the first time in days.

He stood by the big reception desk, talking to one of the night porters. She quickened her steps, hoping that he would not notice her.

He turned at the sound of her step. Their eyes met and he smiled. It was a tentative smile, with more than a hint of rueful apology. Daisy felt miserable enough to be glad of anyone's liking now that she had spurned Gavin's with such finality. She allowed herself to smile back.

Richard covered the ground between them with his swift, athletic stride, looking so relieved, so much like a young puppy who had been too long in disgrace, that Daisy's tender heart was touched.

'Spare me a minute, Daisy.'

There was an unmistakable plea in his eager approach. She paused. 'Hallo, Richard. How are you?'

He brushed aside the niceties of convention. 'I wanted to see you. To apologise! I really am sorry about the other day. I guess I was a little drunk, you know,' he said ruefully.

Daisy felt uncomfortable. She did not want to be reminded. 'Look, I'd rather we didn't talk about it, Richard.'

'I know. But I want you to understand.' He thrust the heavy hair from his forehead in a habitual, slightly nervous gesture. She noticed that it still needed cutting. 'Are you on your way home? Can I walk with you?'

'Aren't you on duty?' She looked at the "bleeper" in his pocket, the personal radio that might summon him to an emergency at any moment.

'Well, I am. But it's reasonably quiet on A and E tonight, or will be until the pubs turn out, anyway. I won't be missed for ten minutes or so.' He pushed open the swing doors for her to pass through, began to descend the wide stone steps by her side. 'I'd like to explain . . .'

Daisy stifled a sigh. 'You don't have to explain, Richard. It's water under the bridge.'

The High Road was never quiet or empty of people for this part of London never seemed to sleep. Sometimes it

was frequented by unsavoury characters, particularly at
night, and Daisy was not too sorry to have his company
as they walked along the pavement towards Clifton
Street.

'I'd been in the pub with some of the lads and there
was a lot of steamy talk about you and Fletcher,' he
persisted in his usual determined fashion. 'I got a bit
worked up, thinking how I'd treated you like a piece of
porcelain for months and then he'd just breezed along
and enjoyed himself with my girl in his usual careless
way. Oh, I know it wasn't like that,' he added hastily as
she stiffened. 'I know you, Daisy. But that's the way it
seemed just then and one thing led to another, I guess.
I've felt rotten ever since—and I've missed you.'

He did sound remorseful. Daisy had liked him and she
had been used to having him around. Suddenly it did not
seem so very terrible that he had lost his head after a few
drinks. And if he did care about her as he claimed then
she must sympathise with the way he had been feeling,
knowing that he had lost her through his own reckless
behaviour.

'I think it's best forgotten. Don't you?' she said with
sudden friendly warmth.

Impulsively, he put his arm about her waist, hugged
her. 'Oh, Daisy! That makes me feel very much better!'
He bent his head to kiss her briefly without any trace of
the passion that had shocked and dismayed her so much.

'Richard! Not in the street!' she protested, half-
laughing. 'What on earth would Matron say?' Drawing
away from him, she saw a sleek silver saloon move away
from the corner of Clifton Street in sudden acceleration.

It was a car that she immediately recognised and her
heart lurched with the fear that Gavin had probably seen

that kiss and her own apparently warm response and put h s own interpretation on the little scene. She wondered bleakly if he had been parked, waiting to intercept her. Or if he had merely been turning out of the side street after calling for Joanne. The car had moved off too quickly for her to see if there was a passenger beside the driver.

'Who cares about Matron!' Richard declared, suddenly light of heart. 'Or anything else as long as we're friends again! We are, aren't we, Daisy?'

It did not seem to matter very much one way or the other. 'If you like,' she agreed without any enthusiasm.

He did not seem to notice that half-hearted assent. 'That's marvellous! It's really been no fun at all without you,' he said earnestly. 'I do care about you, Daisy.'

She glanced up at him, concerned. 'Don't care too much,' she warned. 'Just friends, Richard!'

'Any way you want it,' he promised, a little recklessly. He looked at his watch as they reached the house. 'I have to get back,' he said reluctantly. 'But I'll see you tomorrow?' It was question rather than statement, a little anxious.

Daisy smiled, agreed. Sometimes it was easier to say yes than to argue, she thought wearily, and his boyish diffidence was familiar, even comforting.

Richard hesitated. 'It's Founders's Ball this weekend,' he said, quite unnecessarily in view of the fact that it had been the main topic of conversation among staff at Hartlake for several days. 'I suppose you've already made arrangements?'

'Nothing special.'

'Will you come with me?'

'Why not?' Daisy said brightly. She had not the

slightest chance of going with Gavin. She did not really wish to go at all, but why should she let any man suppose that there was no pleasure for her in anything without him—particularly when it was true!

The flat was empty, but Joanne's special scent lingered. She could only have just gone out—and she had probably gone in Gavin's car, Daisy decided, with a proud little lift to her chin.

Joanne was not important, he had said. But he seemed to be hurtfully quick to console himself with her company, her warm and flattering response to his interest!

Daisy refused to believe that he could have meant any of the things he had said to her . . . because that only made it hurt all the more that he had scooped up her precious chain and gone off with it in a way that implied she would never get it or him back!

CHAPTER THIRTEEN

It was a little rush to get ready. They had been busy on the ward that day and it would have been too much to expect Sister Sweet to allow her juniors to get away early just because they were excited and eager to go to the Ball.

Daisy had a quick shower and scrambled into the flimsy underthings. The very pretty dress of peach organza was laid out in readiness on her bed. Joanne, already dressed in slinky silver lamé that only she could carry off without looking too sexy, helped to build her hair into a cluster of curls high on her head, carefully threaded through with a ribbon to match her dress. Then she slipped the lovely garment over Daisy's head and zipped the long back zip and stood back to admire the effect.

'Very nice,' she said, meaning it. 'You'll be the belle of the Ball.'

Daisy smiled. She knew that no one would notice her when Joanne was in the vicinity, least of all Gavin for whose benefit her friend had dressed with so much care and such obvious provocation, she thought, desperately minding and trying not to show it. 'I was talked into it,' she said lightly. 'But it is pretty, isn't it?'

The dress had cost her far more than she could comfortably afford. She knew that she had been kidding herself at the time that she might go to the Ball with Gavin and so she had not cared what it cost. She had only wanted to please and delight him and the lovely frock really did do something for her hair and face and figure. But that had turned out to be just one more of the many absurd dreams that were doomed to disappointment, she told herself wryly. She would not be dancing in Gavin's arms that evening.

As it happened, she might not be dancing in Richard's arms, either. A last-minute emergency meant that he had to assist with long and complicated surgery on the victim of a road accident. He had telephoned to explain and apologise and promised to try to join her later in the evening if she went with her friends as she had originally planned.

Daisy had been tempted to stay home. It was not going to be much fun to go without an escort and run the risk of being a wallflower while all her girl-friends enjoyed themselves with the man of the moment . . . particularly Joanne.

But, being young and optimistic, she could not be entirely untouched by the infectious excitement all around her. She decided to go to the Ball in her lovely dress and, just like the Cinderella that Gavin had called her, perhaps she would find someone who might not be quite the Prince Charming she wanted so much but a tolerable substitute for the evening.

Gavin was punctual. On such a night, the front door of the house stood open to all comers and so he did not bother to announce his arrival. At his knock on the flat door, Joanne opened it, looking just a little conscious.

'Oh, it's you,' She greeted him with her warm, friendly smile. 'I've been trying to reach you all day.'

He raised an eyebrow. 'I'm not particularly elusive. I've been about the hospital.' He looked beyond the beautiful girl in the clinging silver dress to Daisy, hovering uncertainly in the doorway of the bedroom. 'Is anything wrong?' His tone was absent.

It was obvious to Joanne that her shy friend held much more charm for him than she did. A little satisfaction touched her eyes.

She had been quite unable to shake off the feeling that it would be wrong to come between Daisy and this man. And as Daisy hastily retreated into the bedroom the sudden move confirmed her suspicion. She had evolved a little plan and she was rather pleased to realise that it was going to work out. She had also been very relieved to learn that Richard was not going to be a spanner in the works, after all.

She knew it was dangerous to interfere in such matters, but sometimes it could be forgivable, she felt. Sometimes when two stubborn people were involved a little tactful push went a very long way.

'I've done a dreadful thing,' she announced with no trace of regret. 'I'm double-dated!'

Gavin looked at her with a faint smile about his mouth. 'Oh?'

'Yes. Isn't it awful,' she said blithely. 'I promised days ago that John Seymour could take me tonight—and then forgot! But I can't go back on my word, can I? He did ask me first, you see. You do understand, don't you?'

Gavin's smile deepened. 'Perfectly,' he drawled, carefully not looking towards the hovering figure who had been drawn by Joanne's casual announcement.

Joanne smiled, very warm. 'Then you'll forgive me?' Her golden smile had captivated many men, but she had soon discovered that it had very little real effect on

Gavin Fletcher. It seemed to her that Daisy's shy, sweet smile had much more impact.

'Of course.' He could scarcely do anything but accept the situation and at heart he was relieved. Having asked the girl to go with him, he had felt bound to honour the arrangement, but it was the last thing he had wished.

Daisy suddenly swept into the room, eyes sparkling with indignation on his behalf. She felt it was too bad of Joanne to treat him in such fashion. Any other man— but not Gavin who was more sensitive than most people seemed to understand, she thought protectively.

'You can't do that, Joanne!' she exclaimed reproach- fully. 'It just isn't fair to let someone down at the last moment!'

Gavin's eyes were very warm, very tender as he turned to her. 'Don't worry about me, Daisy,' he said lightly. 'It isn't the first time it's happened.' He smiled at her gently.

Colour flooded her face at the obvious interpretation of her impulsive words—and the painful reminder. Her chin went up and she looked away hastily from the dark eyes with their lurk of gentle laughter.

Her heart moved with sudden love for him. She could not help admiring him for making light of the humilia- tion she had heaped on him. Not many men would forgive and accept—and smile at her in just that way when she had behaved quite unforgivably ever since that first encounter on the ward.

She had been horrid to him, snubbing him, refusing to like or trust him, disappointing him—and then rejecting his gentle and perhaps genuine declaration of love like the spoiled brat that he had once called her! He ought to despise her. She wondered that he could bring himself even to speak to her in that warm and friendly way.

She could forgive him anything because she loved him. But she no longer even dared to dream that he might love her.

'Yes, well . . .' Disconcerted, she turned on Joanne. 'You didn't tell *me* that you were double-dated!'

Joanne shrugged. 'It's been such a rush since you came in that I just haven't had time to tell you anything,' she pointed out smoothly. She smiled at Gavin and said as though it was a sudden inspiration: 'We could make it a foursome! Daisy's date has let her down, too!'

Daisy could have killed her on the spot! She stiffened with outrage and pride. 'I'm sure that Gavin doesn't want to have me thrust on him in such a way,' she said, prickly as a porcupine.

'You might allow Gavin to speak for himself,' he said, smiling. 'I think it's an excellent idea. But we mustn't sweep you into anything you don't wish to do, of course. Perhaps you've already found a replacement for your date?'

'No, but . . .'

'Then that's settled,' Joanne declared with obvious satisfaction. The door-phoned buzzed. 'Now that *is* John! Are you ready, Daisy?' She caught up her wrap and evening bag.

Daisy hesitated, wondering why she felt as though she had been cleverly manipulated by the pair of them.

Gavin said quickly: 'Go on, Joanne. I'll bring Daisy in my car and we'll link up with you later.'

Joanne was gone before Daisy could demur or protest. Her heart was behaving very strangely, leaping all over the place like a wild thing, and she felt breathless.

She wanted more than anything in the world to spend

the evening with Gavin, to dance in his arms and bask in his smiling attentions. But he had been pushed into it by a strangely tactless and unthinking Joanne—and Daisy could not bear to think that he was only sorry for a girl who had, like himself, been unexpectedly let down.

'I'm so sorry,' she said in a little rush. 'Joanne is so impulsive. She just doesn't think and she's so used to everyone falling in with her schemes! But you don't have to feel responsible for me, truly!'

Gavin looked down at her, smiling, refusing to be dismayed by her seeming reluctance to spend the evening in his company. 'I'm very grateful to Joanne,' he said with unmistakable meaning.

Daisy blushed, trembled. Then, confused and embarrassed and fearing that she might throw herself headlong into his arms on a surge of loving, she turned away. 'I'll get my things . . .'

Gavin wondered wryly if she would ever trust him. Without trust, there could be no love, he felt . . . and it had become quite vital to his happiness and his future at Hartlake that she should love him. Nothing mattered quite so much!

When Daisy returned, drawing the flimsy matching stole of peach organza about her slight shoulders, he was standing by the sofa on which the bear that she had christened Edward was still sitting.

Gavin turned, smiling—and from his fingers dangled the gold-coloured ribbon with its distinctive label that had lately adorned the bear's neck. Without a word, he held it out towards her, dancing mischief in his dark eyes.

'If you're looking for a friend, I'd like to apply . . .'

Daisy read the words and looked at him, quite unable

not to smile in swift appreciation and delight. 'You are an idiot!' she declared, rather helplessly.

'I mean it, Daisy.' He was suddenly sober. Being friends with a girl had always been a very minor consideration. Getting her into bed had seemed much more to the point. But Daisy was different. Daisy was his love, his life . . . and perhaps friendship was the only possible starting point for his eventual happiness. 'I've never known anyone like you and so I've made mistakes all the way along the line. I've done and said all the wrong things. Give me one more chance, girl. Let me be your friend, if nothing else.'

She was silent for a moment, checking the impulse to put her arms about him. There had been too many impulses and she seemed to have regretted most of them. Perhaps she should allow her level head to take over from her foolish heart!

She nodded. 'Yes,' she said quietly.

Gavin's heart lifted. But he did not sweep her into his arms as he longed to do. That might be another mistake, he thought wryly. 'The loveliest word in the English language,' he said lightly.

'You've heard it a thousand times,' she reminded him, slightly dry.

'Not on *your* lips, love.' He smiled at her. 'I have the feeling that this is going to be a great evening.'

'That's probably the only yes you'll hear tonight!' she warned him, a little amused.

'That's the only one that matters!' he assured her firmly.

The big hall was crowded with dancing couples and lively parties at the side-tables. Some girls, like Joanne and Daisy, wore long dresses while others wore casual clothes. Some nurses were in uniform, either newly down from the wards or soon to go on duty.

The evening was in full swing when they arrived and everyone seemed to be having a good time. Drinks flowed freely and the music, lively and foot-tapping, had encouraged couples on to the floor.

They found John and Joanne with a group of friends who had pushed three tables together into a premier position close to the dance floor. Daisy tried not to mind the curious glances and murmur of speculation that rippled through the party as she arrived with Gavin.

She was grateful for his light handling of a delicate situation. He had seemed almost impersonal as he escorted her from the flat and down to his car and driven the short distance to the Administration Wing of the hospital. It was a modern block that contained not only the many offices but also the big ballroom that was used for a variety of functions, the staff swimming-pool, indoor squash and tennis courts and the social club that nurses and medical students were encouraged to join although the anti-social shifts of duty were not condu-cive to taking full advantage of its facilities.

The music changed to a slow, dreamy waltz. Most of their party drifted out to the floor. Gavin turned to Daisy, held out his hand. 'I want to show you off,' he said, smiling. 'Every man will be envious of my lovely girl.'

She rose, pleased but refusing to be flattered, knowing the danger of taking him too seriously and yet wishing with all her heart that she could believe the warming glow in his dark eyes, the promise in his smile.

He held her, not too tightly, and his body moved against her own in the slow rhythm of the music and

Daisy sensed the tension and the trembling in his tall, muscular frame. At first, she was stiff, quite unyielding. But gradually the music and the magic in his embrace coaxed the stiffness out of her and she melted, sliding her hand from his broad shoulder to the nape of his neck, encouraging his arm to tighten about her slender waist. She felt a thousand eyes upon them and wondered if it was only imagination or if the whole of Hartlake was agog. His reputation for causing havoc among the nursing staff ought not to endear him to any girl. Daisy simply could not help loving him with all her heart.

They danced like lovers, his cheek pressed hard against her pale hair, unaware of anything but each other, lost in an enchanted world of their own. Time stood still for Daisy and she wanted this magic moment to last for ever and ever.

It was an enchanted evening. Gavin had eyes only for her and did not seem to care if the world knew it. Daisy did not care, either. Perhaps it was only a dream and she would wake to disillusion and despair. Perhaps he did not love her for all the heart-quickening warmth of loving in his touch, his embrace, his response to every word and glance and smile. Daisy loved him and she only wanted him to be happy, only wanted to give him anything and everything he could possibly want for the rest of her life.

With head and heart in a whirl, Daisy nestled against him as he drove her home at the end of the evening with one hand on the wheel, his arm about her in loving, protective embrace. She was drowsy and content and wondering why they couldn't drive to Land's End and back so that this wonderful night need not come to an end too soon.

Gavin brought the car to a standstill outside the house. He bent his head to look into her pretty face, half-hidden against his shoulder. 'Are you asleep, girl?'

'Yes,' she said, a smile hovering.

He chuckled. 'It's time you were in bed.'

'Yes.' She rubbed her cheek against his shoulder affectionately.

He hesitated. Then, eyes dancing, said softly, teasing: 'With me . . .'

Daisy put an arm about his neck and kissed him with her heart on her lips. 'Yes.'

He raised an amused eyebrow. 'Hey! What happened to no?'

She kissed him again. He put both arms about her and drew her against him. Daisy could feel the heavy thud of his heart, the slight quickening of his breath. Her love and her need of him threatened to overwhelm her. 'Take me home, Gavin,' she whispered.

'You are home, love.'

She shook her head with a little impatience for his failure to understand. 'Please . . .'

He hesitated. 'My place?'

'Yes.'

He touched his lips to the soft tendrils of ash-blonde hair that framed her small face. 'No.'

She drew away from him, surprised, a little hurt. 'Don't you want me?'

He smiled wryly. 'Very much.'

She looked into his dark eyes, laid her hand to his lean cheek on a sudden impulse. 'Don't you trust me, Gavin?' she asked gently.

The tables were turned, he thought ruefully. He wondered how to explain his refusal of all that she offered so generously. His body throbbed with longing for her, but he did not just want her in his bed. He wanted her in his life until the end of time—as his dear love and as his wife.

Daisy was troubled by his silence, by the grave look in those usually twinkling eyes. 'I love you,' she said quietly. 'I want you to be happy. I won't disappoint you again, I promise.'

He caught her small, flower-like face in his strong hands, kissed her very tenderly. 'You could never disappoint me, Daisy,' he told her with all the intensity of loving. 'You're all that a man could want in one enchanting package. I love you very much, you know. I want you to marry me.'

She caught her breath on a rapturous tide of delight and incredulity. She had hoped with all her heart, but never dared to dream that he would want to marry her. It was almost too much joy that he should love her as she loved him. 'Oh, Gavin . . . !' she said, almost too full for words.

'Will you marry me?'

'Oh yes!' she said eagerly. 'Yes and yes and yes.'

He reached into his breast pocket and drew out the delicate gold chain that she valued so much. He fastened it about her neck, taking care that the *Yes* side was uppermost on the little gold heart for all the world to see, and her pretty face glowed with wonder and enchantment as he drew her once more into his arms and set the seal on their engagement with a kiss.

Daisy felt that she must be the happiest girl in the world—and certainly she did not think that there could ever have been another nurse with so much reason to bless Hartlake. For her decision to train at the big teaching hospital had led her to the one man in all the world that she had been destined to love with all her heart—and, incredibly, he loved her, too.

To prove it, he wore a little knot of daisies on the lapel of his white coat every day until they were married with as much pride and satisfaction as Daisy wore the gold heart in the hollow of her throat in lieu of an engagement ring.

Two more Doctor Nurse Romances to look out for this month

Mills & Boon Doctor Nurse Romances are proving very popular indeed. Stories range wide throughout the world of medicine – from high-technology modern hospitals to the lonely life of a nurse in a small rural community.

These are the other two titles for March.

HOSPITAL AFFAIR
by Marguerite Lees

Sue Gifford's new job as physiotherapist at a clinic for disabled children seems to clash too often with her boyfriend Keith's needs. And is she imagining that her friendship with Dr Julian Caird has suddenly taken on a new significance?

THE TENDER HEART
by Hazel Fisher

Tender-hearted Nurse Juliet Reed intends devoting her life to caring for the sick. Why then do thoughts of the handsome, brilliant young surgeon Brook Wentworth fill not only her dreams but every waking moment?

On sale where you buy Mills & Boon romances

The Mills & Boon rose is the rose of romance

Look out for these three great Doctor Nurse Romances coming next month

LOVE COMES BY AMBULANCE
by Lisa Cooper

It's common knowledge that the dashing Dr Jason Benedict has no time for the nurses of Beatties – he's in love with a beautiful ballerina. So what chance has Nurse Victoria Lesley of winning his love, especially when he thinks she's a fluffy blonde with no sense?

TEMPESTUOUS APRIL
by Betty Neels

Nurse Harriet Slocombe is invited to spend a holiday at the home of her Dutch friend Sieske. She is stunned when she meets Dr Friso Eysinck, who turns out to be the man of her dreams, but she soon realises that she is not the only girl to have dreams about this particular man.

DOCTOR'S FAMILY
by Clare Cavendish

When her housekeeper aunt gets married the family agrees that Beth must be the one to give up her career and run the house. Beth is heartbroken at having to give up nursing, but can she find compensation in her growing friendship with Dr Jason Bridgeman?

On sale where you buy Mills & Boon romances.

The Mills & Boon rose is the rose of romance

One of the best things in life is...FREE

We're sure you have enjoyed this Mills & Boon romance. So we'd like you to know about the other titles we offer. A world of variety in romance. From the best authors in the world of romance.

The Mills & Boon Reader Service Catalogue lists all the romances that are currently in stock. So if there are any titles that you cannot obtain or have missed in the past, you can get the romances you want DELIVERED DIRECT to your home.

The Reader Service Catalogue is free. Simply send the coupon – or drop us a line asking for the catalogue.

Post to: Mills & Boon Reader Service, P.O. Box 236, Thornton Road, Croydon, Surrey CR9 3RU, England.

*Please note: READERS IN SOUTH AFRICA please write to: Mills & Boon Reader Service of Southern Africa, Private Bag X3010, Randburg 2125, S. Africa.

Please send me my FREE copy of the Mills & Boon Reader Service Catalogue.

NAME (Mrs/Miss) _____ EP1

ADDRESS _____

COUNTY/COUNTRY _____ POST/ZIP CODE _____

BLOCK LETTERS, PLEASE

Mills & Boon
the rose of romance